SPRING FEVER

Standing at the mirror, Jessica applied eyeliner, then backed away to study herself. "I think we're going to have a great time around here: no curfews to worry about, no chores around the house. I just know that Aunt Shirley and Uncle Herman are going to spoil us like crazy. I'll bet they let us do whatever we feel like."

Elizabeth shook her head. "I don't know, Jess. That isn't exactly the impression I got. In fact—"

"Girls!" Mrs. Walker knocked lightly on the door and opened it before either of them could ask her to come in. "Your uncle and I are ready to take you into town now. Have you both freshened up?"

Jessica's eyes widened. The *last* thing she had in mind was going into town with her great-aunt and -uncle!

Bantam Books in the Sweet Valley High Series
Ask your bookseller for the books you have missed

SWEET VALLEY HIGH
Super Edition

SPRING FEVER

Written by
Kate William

Created by
FRANCINE PASCAL

BANTAM BOOKS
TORONTO · NEW YORK · LONDON · SYDNEY · AUCKLAND

RL , IL age 12 and up

SPRING FEVER
A Bantam Book / April 1987

Sweet Valley High is a trademark of Francine Pascal.

Conceived by Francine Pascal.

Produced by Cloverdale Press, Inc.

Cover art by James Mathewuse.

ISBN 0-553-26420-6

Published simultaneously in the United States and Canada

Bantam Books are published by Bantam Books, Inc. Its trademark,
consisting of the words "Bantam Books" and the portrayal of a rooster,
is Registered in U.S. Patent and Trademark Office and in other
countries. Marca Registrada. Bantam Books, Inc., 666 Fifth Avenue,
New York, New York 10103.

PRINTED IN THE UNITED STATES OF AMERICA

O   0 9 8 7 6 5 4 3 2 1

SPRING FEVER

One

"Jessica Wakefield!" Elizabeth called impatiently, knocking for the second time on her sister's closed bedroom door. "Are you going to let me in, or do I have to stand out in the hall all day?"

A second later the door flew open, and Jessica stared at her twin, her blue-green eyes wide with surprise. "I didn't even hear you, Liz," she said, hurrying across the room to turn down her stereo. She wrinkled her nose at the heap of clothing on her unmade bed and tossed her silky blond hair off her shoulders. "What am I going to do?" she wailed dramatically. "I'm never going to be ready to leave tomorrow morning. I'll bet you're all packed and ready to go," she added accusingly.

Identical as they were in appearance, the twins

were polar opposites in behavior. It was a long-standing pattern in the Wakefield household that Elizabeth was always ready in advance, and Jessica was always just late enough to make everyone want to scream.

"I'm almost packed," Elizabeth admitted. She cleared a corner on her sister's bed and sat down. "I can't believe you can even find your suitcase in this mess," she said, giggling. "Jess, at this rate we won't make it to Kansas until spring break's over!"

Jessica pulled her sun-streaked hair back in a ponytail. "I can't believe we're really going to Kansas," she muttered. "I don't want to sound ungrateful or anything, Liz, but don't you honestly think spending eleven days with Uncle Herman and Aunt Shirley is going to be just a little bit dull?"

Elizabeth laughed. One good thing about Jessica was that one always knew where she stood. "I don't think it's going to be dull at all," she said. "Uncle Herman and Aunt Shirley told Mom they've been talking about nothing else since they found out we're coming. I know they'll have millions of things planned for us. Besides, think what fun it'll be to visit a small town in a completely different part of the country."

Jessica sighed. "I don't know," she muttered. "Walkersville, Kansas, doesn't sound all that promising. Lila Fowler's going to Rome with her father," she added in an injured tone.

Elizabeth laughed. Lila Fowler was one of Jessica's closest friends—and one of her biggest rivals. Lila also happened to be the only daughter of one of the wealthiest computer magnates in Southern California. Jetting off to Rome was an ordinary event in the Fowler household.

Elizabeth studied her twin thoughtfully as Jessica took out one of her latest purchases, a white cotton jumpsuit studded with tiny rhinestones. It was hard for Elizabeth to imagine being jealous of Lila Fowler or even thinking about spending six months allowance on an outfit that would go out of style in less than six minutes. But there was no explaining differences in taste. Jessica couldn't help the way she was any more than Elizabeth could. It just made Elizabeth chuckle sometimes to think that they could be identical in appearance and behave so very differently.

Sixteen years old and slender, the twins had sun-streaked, shoulder-length blond hair. Their wide-set eyes were the dazzling blue-green of the Pacific. With the exception of a mole on

Elizabeth's right shoulder, every physical detail was identical, down to the dimple each showed when she smiled. "Clones," Steven, their eighteen-year-old brother, liked to call them. And while they were growing up they had heard every possible variation on that theme. They had been called carbon copies, double images, the ditto sisters, every possible name. But anyone who knew Elizabeth or Jessica very well could tell them apart instantly.

It wasn't just a question of style and fashion, though that helped identify them. Jessica's nickname might as well be "Fad." Whatever the newest craze was, Jessica knew about it. She read magazines by the armful every month, anxious to learn about the newest in everything from hairstyles and makeup to dance steps, swimwear, movie stars, and music. The newer something was, the better Jessica liked it.

It was true Jessica had never dated the same boy for very long, or stuck with one of her hobbies long enough to see it through. Of course, the things that mattered most to her remained constant. Cheerleading, being president of Pi Beta Alpha, an exclusive sorority at Sweet Valley High, dancing for hours at the Beach Disco: these things Jessica would never give up.

Elizabeth knew "steady" was a fair word to describe herself. She was as responsible and hardworking as her twin was flighty and fickle. It wasn't just that Elizabeth preferred muted colors and conservative clothing, either. She liked to completely devote herself to ideas and activities one at a time. And she had *one* best friend, Enid Rollins, and *one* steady boyfriend, Jeffrey French. Not that Elizabeth didn't have lots of other friends, but she was essentially a private person and didn't enjoy crowds or big parties as much as Jessica did.

Elizabeth had always dreamed of being a writer. She knew that to realize her ambition she would have to work hard, be disciplined, and learn to be a good listener. As a writer she would have to be perceptive and diligent, two traits Elizabeth hoped she had already acquired. She wrote as much as possible, devoting a lot of her time to *The Oracle*, Sweet Valley High's school paper.

Elizabeth's thoughts were interrupted by a knock on Jessica's bedroom door.

"Come in," Jessica called.

"Oh, good. You're both here," Mrs. Wakefield said, coming into the room and giving her daughters a sunny smile. Neat, pert, and blue eyed, Alice Wakefield didn't look that much older than the twins. She could still fit into their size six clothing, too. That day she had managed to take the afternoon off from her interior design business so she could help the girls get ready. "I've got some last-minute things to go over with you two," she added, frowning as she regarded the open suitcase on Jessica's bed. "Jess, I thought you and I had agreed that *conservative* things are best for Walkersville," she said, picking up the white cotton jumpsuit.

Jessica snatched the jumpsuit from her mother. "There's nothing wrong with this," she assured her. "It's perfectly simple, Mom." She looked mournfully at the little rhinestone studs. "You should see some of the things Lila's taking to Rome. She got the neatest red leather miniskirt, and this pair of boots with purple fringe, and—"

"Walkersville is not Rome, Jess," Mrs. Wakefield said with a shake of her head. "Now, I mean it, you two. You have to remember that Uncle Herman and Aunt Shirley are a whole generation older than Dad and I. They're in their sixties, Grandma and Grandpa's age."

"We understand," Elizabeth said, giving her twin a dirty look. "Honestly, Mom, we're not going to do anything to upset them. We promise."

Mrs. Wakefield still looked uneasy. "You know, when I had the idea for this trip of yours I was remembering what a wonderful visit I had when I went out to Walkersville for a few weeks." She smiled, looking reminiscent. "I was exactly the age you two are now, and I had never been to a small town before. I fell madly in love with Walkersville. It's so quaint—so quiet. It looked like something in a fairy-tale to me."

"I know we're going to love it, too," Elizabeth said, giving her mother a hug. "And we're really excited about seeing Aunt Shirley and Uncle Herman again. We haven't seen them since we were ten!"

"They're real pillars of society in Walkersville," Mrs. Wakefield mused. "After all, the town was originally founded by Uncle Herman's grandfather. And now Uncle Herman's the mayor. And I don't think there's a single committee that your great-aunt isn't on. Everyone looks up to them." She smiled. "I know you two will get VIP treatment, but by the same token you're going to be in the limelight. You'll have to do things the way they do in Kansas. Remember, when in Rome, do as the Romans do. And when in Walkersville—"

"Do as the Walkers do!" Elizabeth finished for her.

Jessica, who was busily sneaking her jumpsuit back into her suitcase, didn't look quite as enthusiastic at the prospect of adapting her behavior to Walkersville rules. "I'm sure Liz and I will liven things up," she said cheerfully. "It can't be *that* boring," she added. "There have to be some cute guys *some*where."

Mrs. Wakefield burst out laughing. "Well, if there are, I'm sure you'll find them," she remarked. "But remember, you two, whatever Aunt Shirley and Uncle Herman say, goes. No talking back to them, OK?"

"OK, Mom," Elizabeth said.

"Jess," Mrs. Wakefield said sternly.

"OK, OK," Jessica said hastily, rummaging through her collection of headbands for ones the right colors to go with the clothes she'd selected.

"Mom's right," Elizabeth announced when their mother had left the room. "We're really going to have to be careful, Jess. It sounds like Aunt Shirley and Uncle Herman aren't used to teenagers."

"Oh, we'll break them in," Jessica said cheerfully, taking out a pair of enormous plastic ear-

8

rings. "Aren't these great? I found them at the mall," she said, holding them up to her ears. "I hope they'll be a hit in Walkersville."

"I think Walkersville sounds wonderful," Elizabeth said dreamily, staring out Jessica's window at the lush California foliage. "I've always wanted to go to a little midwestern town. I bet people are really friendly there."

"You think they have tornadoes all the time, like in *The Wizard of Oz*?" Jessica asked hopefully.

Elizabeth laughed. "Not in April, silly," she scoffed. She shook her head at her twin. "Can't you look forward to a nice, peaceful visit? I don't know about you, Jess, but I'm really ready for some peace and quiet."

Jessica stared at her twin. "No one goes on vacation for peace and quiet, Liz," she said reprovingly. "Not unless you're middle-aged or something. The point of a vacation is to have *fun*."

Elizabeth couldn't help giggling at the shocked expression on her twin's face. Clearly the thought of relaxing sent her sister into a panic.

Jessica would just have to get used to a slower life-style on their vacation. As far as Elizabeth was concerned, a slower life-style was exactly what she and her twin sister needed. And, she hoped, Walkersville, Kansas, would be the perfect place for all the rest she required. Not even the prospect of saying goodbye to Jeffrey for eleven days could dim Elizabeth's anticipation.

She couldn't wait to get to her aunt and uncle's. And, she thought, the very next day their vacation began!

Two

"Do you see them anywhere?" Elizabeth whispered anxiously to her sister as they peered around the crowded waiting area outside gate six in the airport.

"Look! There they are!" Jessica exclaimed, spotting the couple hurrying toward them, their faces lit up with welcoming smiles. The next minute confusion broke loose as they all tried to hug one another at once. "Good heavens, would you just look at these two!" Mrs. Walker exclaimed. She backed off to shake her head at the twins. "Herman, they're all grown up!"

The twins' aunt and uncle looked almost exactly the way Elizabeth and Jessica remembered. Their great-aunt was a petite woman in her early sixties, her dark hair peppered with silver

11

and her almond-shaped eyes a lovely shade of blue. Laugh lines showed around her eyes and mouth when she smiled, making her look warm and kind, just as the twins thought a great-aunt should look! She was dressed in a stylish suit, and her manner was very proper. She even wore a tiny blue hat to match her shoes. Their great-uncle, who had a hearty, booming voice that the twins loved, was a slightly portly man in his midsixties, his hair and mustache silver-gray. He was wearing a suit, too, and the twins suppressed giggles as they exchanged knowing glances. On the plane they had agreed that their great-uncle would probably look like the mayor of a small town wherever he went, even if it was just to the airport to pick up his great-nieces. They both felt proud, though, of their great-aunt and great-uncle. And they couldn't wait to get to know them both!

"We have so much to catch up on, girls," Mrs. Walker said as if she were reading their minds. "I just can't get over you two," she added, her eyes misting over a little. "Seeing you two now, it reminds me of the time your mother came out to stay with us. It seems like yesterday, doesn't it, Herman?"

Putting an arm around each twin's shoulder,

their uncle nodded. "You'll have to forgive us if we sound like antiques from time to time," he said affectionately. "We're not used to having young ladies come to stay with us."

"We've been counting the minutes till your arrival," his wife added happily. "I didn't sleep one wink last night, I was so excited. Tell us how your flight was," she added, leaning over to flick an invisible speck of lint from Jessica's sweater.

Elizabeth bit her lip to keep from smiling. She couldn't believe how patiently Jessica was putting up with her aunt's fussiness. "The flight was perfect," Elizabeth answered. Jessica was too busy staring at the airport around them to respond.

"We want to know everything about Kansas and Walkersville," Jessica told her aunt. "Don't we, Liz? Mom and Dad are always telling me how much more open and friendly people are out here. Is that really true?"

"Well, you'll probably find Walkersville quite a surprise after Sweet Valley," Mrs. Walker said as they headed down to the baggage claim area. "It's really quite a sleepy little town. Of course everyone knows everyone else. I suppose we really *are* quite friendly, come to think of it."

13

"Are there lots of kids our age?" Jessica asked eagerly.

Mr. Walker laughed heartily. "There sure are. In fact, something tells me you girls will be getting quite a reception. We've been talking about your visit for a long time now, and everyone between the age of fifteen and twenty has been properly alerted. I bet you'll have so many invitations you won't know what to do with yourselves!"

Jessica's eyes shone. Elizabeth couldn't resist giggling a little. She knew Jessica had only one kind of invitation in mind, an invitation from someone about six feet tall, handsome, and lots of fun—the midwestern boy she was determined to meet and fall madly in love with. Something told her that their aunt and uncle had a different kind of reception in mind!

By now the four of them had reached the baggage claim area, and they spent the next ten minutes trying to identify and wrestle with the twins' luggage. Elizabeth had brought one good-size bag, which she found right away. But Jessica had insisted on bringing her entire set of luggage, four pieces, and her dress bag was the very last piece off the plane. "It looks like you'll be very well equipped," her aunt said with a smile, lifting one of Jessica's bags. "I hope you won't be disappointed, Jessica, if there aren't too many places to wear all your pretty clothes."

Jessica looked horrified, but when Elizabeth nudged her sharply in the ribs she managed a shaky smile. "Oh, I really didn't bring anything special," she lied. "Just a few old rags."

Then it was their aunt's turn to look dismayed. "Of course, there will be *some* functions. I know for a fact that my dear friend Lily Sawyer wants to have you girls out to her farm for a day. And then there's the big square dance coming up a week from Sunday and—"

"Don't listen to my sister," Elizabeth said reassuringly, tucking her arm through her aunt's. "One thing you can count on is that wherever you take Jessica, she'll have at least three or four outfits for the occasion."

Mrs. Walker smiled, looking slightly puzzled. Elizabeth patted her arm, noticing that Jessica was already busy staring at a cute, auburn-haired skycap, who was wrestling with an elderly woman's suitcase. A frown crossed Elizabeth's face. Was Jessica going to be able to behave herself during their vacation? Something told her that it wasn't very likely. Their aunt and uncle seemed very set in their ways. They

15

weren't used to teenage girls, and it would probably be quite an adjustment having two sixteen-year-olds to contend with.

Elizabeth hoped Jessica would be sensitive enough to tone her actions and dress down just a little. Otherwise, she didn't see how they could possibly avoid conflicts during their visit, especially since Jessica seemed determined to make Kansas as lively as possible.

Elizabeth also hoped that their aunt and uncle had enough activities planned to keep Jessica out of trouble, or there was no telling what shape Walkersville would be in by the time the twins departed!

"It's so beautiful!" Jessica exclaimed. The twins were in the backseat of their uncle's navy blue Chevrolet, looking around as they drove down the highway and away from the airport. The plains around them stretched as far as they could see. "I've never seen anything so flat before!" Jessica added, her eyes wide.

"It's certainly flat," her aunt agreed. "And you're right. It is also beautiful."

"It looks just like I always pictured it when I read about the pioneers moving west," Elizabeth murmured, enchanted. The early-spring fields stretched around them on all sides, a soft, celery color. Here and there groups of cattle grazed together in pastures. The blue of the sky was soft and luminous. The landscape was so peaceful and lovely Elizabeth thought she knew then what her mother meant about the magic of that part of the country. "I'm so glad we've come," she said impulsively.

Jessica nodded, round-eyed. "Me, too," she said.

"Well, sit back and enjoy the scenery," their uncle suggested, "because we've got a long ride ahead to Walkersville!"

To Elizabeth, though, it seemed that the next hour flew by. There was so much to catch up on! Though their aunt and uncle did correspond frequently by phone and letter, there was really no substitute for a visit. They wanted to hear everything about Steven—how he liked college, whether he had a girlfriend, what kind of career he was planning. Once the twins had assured their aunt and uncle that he loved college, had a wonderful girlfriend, Cora Walker—whose last name was coincidentally the same as their aunt and uncle's—and that he still had no ideas about his long-term career plans, the conversation turned back to the twins.

"What about you girls? You must be too young to be worrying about boyfriends," Mrs. Walker said from the front seat.

The twins exchanged looks. "Well, actually, there *is* a guy who's a special friend of mine back home," Elizabeth said slowly. "His name is Jeffrey French, and he's—" She stopped and looked uncertainly at Jessica. Would her aunt and uncle understand how she felt about Jeffrey? It didn't seem likely. Her aunt was looking at her with a bemused expression on her face.

"But aren't you a little young to get serious about any one boy?" her aunt pressed her.

"Shirley," her husband said reprovingly.

Mrs. Walker blushed a little. "You two have to forgive me," she said quickly. "I forget how long it's been since we've had girls your age around the house! What about you, Jessica?" she added. "Do you have a boyfriend, too?"

Jessica shook her head vigorously. "No," she assured her aunt. "I hate to get tied down," she added self-righteously, avoiding her sister's gaze as she sat up straighter. "I think I'm much too young to get attached to anyone," she added in a voice Elizabeth had never heard before.

Elizabeth gave her a dirty look, but Jessica was just hitting her stride. Soon she and their aunt were agreeing vehemently on the dangers of going steady in high school. Elizabeth listened in disbelief. Jessica was too much sometimes, she thought. True, Jessica really wasn't serious about anyone. But that wasn't because she considered herself too young. It was just that Jessica got bored too easily to allow any of her crushes to develop into anything meaningful. *Just wait*, Elizabeth thought uneasily. Jessica and their aunt sounded as though they were on the same wavelength then—but what would happen when Jessica developed one of her mad crushes in Walkersville, and gave their aunt a chance to see just what "not getting serious" really meant?

But she didn't have time to continue her reflections. "We're coming into Walkersville," the twins' uncle exclaimed, turning off the highway onto a two-lane paved road. The twins craned their necks, eager for their first view of the town. Elizabeth couldn't believe it as they approached the first white clapboard houses. And then they were on Main Street, which looked exactly like something in a storybook. It was a wide, sleepy avenue lined with high, arching trees. A white church with a tall steeple marked one end of the street. There was a white brick town hall building near the other end. Between there were some clothing stores, a big five-and-ten called Walker's, one movie theater, a supermarket, and a few specialty stores. As people passed the Walkers' car on foot or on bicycles, they called out greetings. Everyone really did seem to know everyone else.

"It's such a sweet little town!" Jessica cried, hanging out the window for a better view. "And that's your store, right?" Jessica said, pointing to the five-and-dime.

"It sure is!" Mr. Walker laughed. "Though I'm afraid I'm too busy these days to run it myself. A man named John Campbell takes care of it for me most of the time now. It's a good old-fashioned five-and-ten-cent store, with a real soda fountain inside. It's a popular hangout for the teenagers in town," he added.

Jessica's eyes shone as she spotted a group of three or four guys in front of the dime store. "Maybe Liz and I can help you out by working behind the soda fountain one day," she suggested slyly.

"What a thoughtful idea, Jessica." Her aunt beamed. "Our house is about six blocks from the center of town," she added as they drove down Main Street and turned left onto a narrow road. "You girls can use the bicycles we have in the shed if you like. It's a nice way to enjoy the scenery while you go into town."

"That sounds great," Jessica murmured. Elizabeth was too intent on the lovely old houses lining the street to respond. Suddenly the excitement of being in a new place overcame her. Eleven whole days in a lovely little town with no schoolwork to worry about, no responsibilities, nothing to think about but having a good time, getting to know her great-aunt and uncle, and learning everything they could about life in a small town! Her eyes shone as she stared out the window. She could hardly believe it when her uncle said, "Well, here we are!" a few minutes later.

A small sign that said Five Elms was hanging on a tree at the end of the Walkers' long gravel drive. The house was charming, a rambling old Victorian, painted light gray with white shutters. It had a huge, open, wraparound porch. The house was set back a couple of hundred feet from the street, and the twins kept saying over and over again how strange it felt to have so much *space* around them. "It's like we're the only people around for miles!" Jessica exclaimed, jumping out of the car.

Mr. and Mrs. Walker smiled fondly at each other. Clearly they were proud of Five Elms, and it was a great joy to them to show the girls around. And it was a house to be proud of. The porch was filled with white wicker chairs, some of them rockers. A cat was asleep in one of the chairs, and a tangle of kittens was sleeping on a braided rug on the wooden porch floor. The twins' uncle opened the screen door and the heavy white door behind it, then let the girls inside. They couldn't help gasping at what they saw. Room after room was filled with charming old country furniture, and all the walls were papered in delicate, old-fashioned prints. The kitchen looked like something in a magazine, all red brick with copper pots and pans hanging from iron hooks, and a huge brick fireplace that really worked!

"Let me show you your room," their aunt said, smiling. "We have three bedrooms upstairs, but we thought you two might prefer sharing the back room down here." She smiled shyly. "It's the room your mother stayed in when she came out here to visit."

"Oh, Aunt Shirley, it's perfect," the twins

said in unison when she opened the door. The room looked onto the wraparound porch toward the back of the house. Beams ran along the ceiling and gave the room the appearance of a cozy attic room. The twin beds were covered with faded patchwork quilts, and a small sampler hung over each bed.

"It's so beautiful!" Elizabeth said. "Aunt Shirley, what a wonderful place Five Elms is!"

They were finally in Walkersville, Elizabeth thought, and it was perfect. Absolutely perfect. The setting was every bit as enchanting as their mother had promised them, and now they were both ready to unpack their things and see the town.

Walkersville was only six blocks away. And the twins had a lot of exploring to do.

Three

"I can't wait to go into town!" Jessica exclaimed, whirling around from the mirror with her hairbrush in her hand. "Did you see that guy in front of Walker's when we drove past, that really tall one with the sandy-colored hair? Liz, he was *so* cute!"

Elizabeth laughed and reached for her turquoise sweater. "Jess, I think you're going to have to calm down a little," she said reprovingly. "You saw Aunt Shirley's expression when I started talking about Jeffrey. She doesn't think we're old enough to date."

"Oh, she can't possibly mean that," Jessica said dismissively. "She and Uncle Herman seem really sweet, Liz. I can't imagine them giving us a hard time." She applied some eyeliner around her eyes, then backed away to study herself. "In fact, I think we're going to have a great time here: no curfews to worry about, no chores around the house . . . I can just tell Aunt Shirley and Uncle Herman are going to be the sort who spoil us like crazy. I'll bet they let us do whatever we feel like."

Elizabeth shook her head. "I don't know, Jess. That isn't exactly the impression I got. In fact—"

"Girls!" Mrs. Walker exclaimed, knocking lightly on the door and opening it before either of them could ask her to come in. "Your uncle and I are ready to take you into town now! Have you both freshened up?"

Jessica's eyes widened. The last thing she had in mind was going into town with her aunt and uncle. The whole point was for her and Elizabeth to look around on their own, to see if those guys were still hanging out in front of Walker's. "Uh—you and Uncle Herman must be tired after driving all the way out to the airport and back," she said. "Why don't you stay home and relax? Liz and I can wander into town on our own and just—"

"Good heavens, we wouldn't dream of sending you off alone," her aunt said, looking hurt. "We want to give you a tour!"

Jessica bit her lip and stared at Elizabeth. "I—uh, that's—uh, that's really nice of you," she concluded helplessly.

"We'll be waiting for you out front," their aunt said happily, pulling the door closed behind her.

"What did I tell you?" Elizabeth said, giggling at the infuriated expression on her sister's face. "Come on, it won't be that bad," she assured her. "Besides, something tells me we're going to have to get used to doing a lot of things differently here than we do at home. And there's no time like the present for adjusting!"

"I don't know about that," Jessica muttered grimly. "There's no way I'm going to spend my whole spring vacation trailing around after Aunt Shirley and Uncle Herman." A mischievous little smile played across her lips. "After all, Walkersville can't be *that* complicated. Once we get to know our way around, I'm sure we'll be able to figure out some way to get them to give us more freedom."

Elizabeth didn't answer. Secretly she thought her sister was off the mark. But she didn't see what good it would do to share her misgivings on their very first day there.

*   *   *

"What an adorable town!" Jessica cried. One thing was certain. She loved Main Street. It was a little like being in a time warp. Everything looked slightly out-of-date, as if time had frozen and things remained exactly as they were ten years earlier. The styles in the clothing stores were out-of-date, and Jessica, always ahead of fashion, even in stylish Sweet Valley, couldn't help feeling a little bit like a movie star as they walked down the street. She could tell people were gaping at her and Elizabeth. *And why not?* she thought immodestly. She knew she stood out in her tight black stirrup pants, bright raspberry T-shirt, and black, man-tailored jacket she was wearing. Her pointy black sunglasses completed the look, though her aunt looked pained when she put them on.

"Jessica, dear, don't you think those sunglasses are a little—uh, a little—"

"Aren't they outrageous?" Jessica filled in for her, digging around in her purse for some chewing gum. She found a pack and offered it around, much to Elizabeth's amusement.

"No, thank you," her aunt and uncle said, giving each other startled looks.

"I just want to run across the street and look in the window of that sweet little craft shop,"

28

Jessica announced, winking at Elizabeth. "Why don't the three of you go on, and I'll meet you up at the church in just a couple of minutes?"

Shirley Walker patted her hair, a gesture the twins were quickly recognizing as a sign of consternation. "Well," she said, looking slightly alarmed, "I suppose—"

But there was no stopping Jessica, who was already across the street. Elizabeth did her best to reassure her aunt and uncle as they continued up the street without her twin. *Jessica definitely owes me one*, she thought to herself, slipping her arm through her aunt's. She then listened patiently to a description of the town's history.

Jessica waited until they were half a block ahead of her before strolling toward Walker's, where she had spied the group of guys earlier. They were still in evidence, and they were watching her with enormous curiosity. Just as she reached them Jessica pulled her hair back with both hands and looked them over, frankly enjoying their attention. They were staring at her as if she were some kind of celebrity.

"Do any of you guys know what time it is?" Jessica asked finally, when the silence was beginning to feel oppressive. The tall, really cute boy turned red as if she had just proposed to him.

"It's almost three," he said shyly, smiling straight at her. "You must be one of the Walkers' nieces," he added.

Jessica tossed her head. "That's right," she said, giving him her most flirtatious smile. Jessica was having fun! For the first time she wasn't envious of Lila's being in Rome. It was so much more fun standing out and getting attention. She was sure Lila wasn't getting that much attention in such a large city!

"My name is Dennis," the tall boy said, scratching his head a little. "Dennis Stevens. We've all been really looking forward to meeting you and your sister," he added sincerely.

"That's so sweet of you," Jessica said, putting out her hand to shake his. She got a special kick out of watching his face redden when she touched him. Next she was introduced to Dennis's four friends, Sam, Matthew, Hank, and Louis. They all seemed nice, but Jessica couldn't get over how tongue-tied and nervous they all were. They couldn't believe she was really from California. One of them even asked her if she ever met any movie stars and if it was really always sunny out there. Jessica couldn't resist making Sweet Valley sound even more glamorous than it was. Within minutes she had the group of boys transfixed, especially Dennis, who was listening with a rapt expression on his face.

"Hey, look," Hank said suddenly, pointing down the street. "It's Annie Sue and Mary."

Shoving both hands in his pockets Dennis blushed and looked around anxiously. Jessica stared at him, trying to figure out why his behavior had changed so suddenly. Then, turning to watch the two girls coming toward them, she quickly put two and two together. The taller of the two was a lithe brunette. From the expression on her face it was clear she was angry about something, and from the way she was staring at Jessica, it was pretty clear what that something—or someone—was.

"Uh-oh," Louis said under his breath. "Annie Sue looks like she's pretty mad, Dennis."

Dennis shrugged, but Jessica thought he looked pale. The girl next to Annie Sue was a small, plump blond with blue eyes. She looked passive beside Annie Sue, definitely the follower, Jessica thought. Annie Sue marched right up to the group and stared coldly at Jessica. "You," she said in an unfriendly voice, "must be the Walkers' niece. Which one are you?"

Jessica stared at her. She couldn't remember anyone being so deliberately unfriendly to her before. This girl's voice was like ice! "I'm Jessica," she said coolly. "Jessica Wakefield. Who are you?"

"Annie Sue Sawyer," the girl said, tossing her head and looking as though Jessica ought to recognize her name instantly.

"Oh," Jessica said, still baffled. "It's nice to meet you." She smiled as winningly as she could under the circumstances and put out her hand.

Annie Sue didn't take her hand; she gave her a dirty look instead. "I suppose you think Walkersville is pretty small and boring compared to Hollywood or wherever you're from," she said in a high, unfriendly voice.

Jessica blinked. She didn't know what kind of impression Annie Sue had managed to get of the twins in advance, but it obviously wasn't a very good one. "I think Walkersville is wonderful," she said honestly. "We're not from Hollywood, either. We're from Sweet Valley, which really isn't that big a town. Bigger than this, I mean, but—"

Annie Sue tucked her arm possessively through Dennis's and regarded Jessica with obvious distaste. "I'm sure it's a great place," she said flatly, clearly signaling that the discussion was over. She turned to Dennis then, her expression changing completely. "I'm so glad I ran into you, Den," she purred, stroking his arm with her hand. "I just want to tell you how excited I am about that little party you guys are throwing tonight." She glanced at Jessica out of the corner of her eyes. "It sounds like it's going to be so much *fun*."

Jessica bit her lip uncomfortably. She couldn't believe Annie Sue was being so rude. It just didn't make sense. Why mention a party when she obviously had no intention of asking Jessica to come? Jessica had never met anyone who seemed to take such an instant dislike to her. It made her feel very peculiar, and she couldn't think of a single thing to do or say.

Dennis, still blushing, looked apologetically at Jessica. "It's just a really tiny, little party," he said by way of explanation, shifting his weight from one foot to the other. "If we'd known when you girls were coming . . ."

"You don't have to make apologies, Dennis," Annie Sue interrupted, giving Jessica a frosty smile. "I'm sure Jessica and her sister have much better things to do, anyway. Come on, honey.

Let's go inside and get that hot fudge sundae you've been promising me." She turned to the other girl. "Come on, Mary."

Dennis sighed heavily. "Well, it's been nice meeting you," he said, smiling at Jessica as if he really meant it. "I hope I get to see you again really soon."

Not knowing what else to do, Jessica said goodbye to the boys and began walking up the street. It was weird! No doubt about it, Jessica thought as she hurried to meet Elizabeth and her aunt and uncle at the church, something strange was going on in Walkersville. She couldn't get over how unfriendly the girls had been. That certainly wasn't the sort of reception she had expected, and she couldn't help wondering what was the cause of their reception.

"Aunt Shirley, do you see that girl standing in front of the craft shop?" Jessica asked. It was late afternoon now, and the twins and their aunt and uncle were strolling back through town together, their tour completed. Jessica hadn't gotten a chance to describe her strange encounter to Elizabeth before she spotted Annie Sue,

34

alone now, standing in front of the store and glancing anxiously at her watch.

"Why, that's Annie Sue Sawyer, one of the sweetest girls in town," Mrs. Walker said with a big smile. "Remember, I mentioned the Sawyers' farm to you earlier? Annie Sue's grandmother is the one who owns it. She's one of my very dearest friends. We've been talking for months about how wonderful it will be when you girls all get a chance to know one another." She beamed. "We just know you're going to get to be good friends as soon as you meet."

Jessica stared at the tall brunette, her confusion growing. So Annie Sue had been encouraged to welcome the twins—yet she had snubbed Jessica when they met. Jessica couldn't figure it out.

"Let's go over, and I'll introduce you to her," Mrs. Walker was saying before Jessica had a chance to explain that she and Annie Sue had already met. "Annie Sue!" she called, waving her arm in greeting. "Come and meet the twins!"

Annie Sue consulted her watch, looking much less excited than Shirley Walker at the prospect. "Jessica and I have already met," she said coolly, coming forward with a strained smile on her face. "Haven't we?" she added, turning to look directly at Jessica.

"Have you? Jessica, dear, you didn't say anything about it," her aunt said with gentle reproachfulness. "Well, this is Elizabeth, Jessica's twin sister. Elizabeth, this is Annie Sue Sawyer." Mrs. Walker looked hopefully at the three girls. "Maybe we should go off and leave you three together, to get better acquainted," she suggested.

"Oh, I really can't, Mrs. Walker," Annie Sue said, trying to look sorry about it. "I'm supposed to meet Dennis here, and we've got to run a couple of errands. But it's nice to meet you. I'm sure we'll run into each other again soon," she said dutifully to Elizabeth. "And nice to see you again," she added to Jessica, managing to convey the opposite sentiment with her flat tone.

"Isn't she adorable?" Mrs. Walker gushed when Annie Sue had crossed the street, leaving the four of them alone again. Jessica and Elizabeth exchanged glances.

"Very sweet," Jessica echoed with a wince.

She decided then and there that either her aunt was a bad judge of character or she just wanted to believe the best about Annie Sue, because there was no denying Annie Sue Sawyer was anything but pleased that Jessica and Elizabeth had arrived in town.

"It's weird, that's what it is," Jessica announced, tossing down the latest issue of *Vogue* and fixing her twin with a piercing gaze. It was their first night in their new room, and Elizabeth was relaxing in the wicker armchair in the corner, rifling absently through the local newspaper, *The Gazette.*

"I know what you mean," Elizabeth agreed. "Everywhere we went today the guys looked happy that we stopped to say hello, but the girls looked as if they were ready to murder us!"

"Especially that Annie Sue creature," Jessica muttered. "Boy, she's really got her claws out, to borrow an expression from Mom. She acted as if she wanted to kill me just because I said four or five words to her boyfriend."

"Well, maybe they're threatened," Elizabeth mused. "I mean, look at it from their point of view. It's such a small town, and everyone knows everyone else. Maybe they're worried that two out-of-towners will throw things off balance."

37

"Yeah, maybe," Jessica agreed. "She was so snippy about our being from California. Like we're some pair of stuck-up movie stars or something who are coming out here to steal her boyfriend." She giggled. "Though Dennis *is* kind of cute. Maybe I should give Annie Sue something to really worry about!"

"Jess," Elizabeth said, warning her twin. "I'll tell you what really worries me. Aunt Shirley seems to have blinders on when it comes to the Walkersville girls. I get the impression she's planning on nothing short of chummy pajama parties. And Annie Sue looked like she couldn't even stand talking to us for five minutes!"

"*I* think we should give this Annie Sue exactly what she expects," Jessica declared. "If she expects us to act like stuck-up brats, maybe that's just how we *should* act!"

"You didn't let me finish," Elizabeth objected. "I was going to say that what worries me is hurting Aunt Shirley. Remember, we promised Mom that we'd be sensitive—on our best behavior, right?"

"I guess so," Jessica sighed.

"Well, I'm afraid that might mean being patient with the girls in town, at least until we get a better idea of why they're so down on us," Elizabeth said.

"I have a feeling that Annie Sue is the leader around here," Jessica said. "And if that's true, everyone will do what she wants them to do." She was silent for a moment. "Well, we could try killing her and Mary with kindness," she mused. "You know, just try to charm them to death. They can't stay icy for long if we really try to be friends with them."

"That sounds like the best way to go," Elizabeth said thoughtfully. She wasn't so sure they would succeed. But Jessica was right, she supposed. All they could really do was give it a try.

Four

"Mmmmm," Jessica said, helping herself to a third blueberry pancake and dousing it with fresh maple syrup. "I could sure get used to eating this kind of breakfast every day!"

"I can't tell you girls what a pleasure it is to have you here," their aunt said fondly, setting a carton of milk down on the table. They were having a late Sunday breakfast after church in the dining nook of the big kitchen. The twins had been in Walkersville for three days and already certain things had become fixed habits, such as long, leisurely breakfasts while their uncle read snippets aloud from *The Gazette*. That morning was no exception. Mr. Walker had his reading glasses on, and he glanced up at the twins with a smile. "Girls, you're in luck," he declared. "The carnival will be in town for the next week."

"Carnival?" Elizabeth and Jessica said, raising their eyebrows at each other.

Mr. Walker nodded, still scanning the Sunday paper. "It's right here in the paper," he said, smiling. "I knew it was going to be coming, but I wanted it to be a surprise for you. The carnival will be in town for a week, starting today at five o'clock."

"Today!" Jessica exclaimed. "That's wonderful!"

Their aunt laughed at the excited looks on their faces. "It doesn't take long for you girls to get caught up in Walkersville traditions," she said affectionately. "The carnival is fun, but don't get your hopes up too high," she added. "It's just a small town carnival, nothing elaborate."

But the twins didn't hear her. They were too excited. A carnival! "Can we go tonight?" Jessica asked, jumping up from the breakfast table. She was already imagining how great she would look strolling casually up to the first tent. All the guys would faint when they saw her in her new jumpsuit with the rhinestone studs. She had never been to a real carnival before, and she was sure it would be fantastic.

42

"Of course we can go," Mrs. Walker said, smiling. "But, girls—"

She never had time to finish her sentence. Jessica had grabbed Elizabeth by the hand and yanked her out of her chair. "Let's go figure out what we're going to wear!" she shrieked. Elizabeth burst out laughing, allowing herself to be dragged from the room. "There's no one like Jessica when she gets excited about something," she said, giggling. Clearly the carnival was one of those things. And there wasn't going to be a single minute of peace and quiet until the twins had gone to the carnival to check it out for themselves.

"I don't know, Jess," Elizabeth said, frowning. "Don't you think that's a little—I don't know—a little *much* for Walkersville?" The twins were getting dressed for the carnival after an afternoon of exploring the neighboring countryside.

Jessica spun around in front of the mirror, her expression indignant. "I think it's just perfect," she said with a sniff, tossing back her sun-streaked hair and admiring her reflection.

43

The jumpsuit fit her perfectly, and her white leather boots set the outfit off spectacularly.

"You look like someone on a game show." Elizabeth giggled. Her own choice of clothes was considerably more subdued, a plaid wrap skirt and cotton sweater. "I can't believe you're so excited about this carnival, Jess," she added. "It doesn't really seem like your kind of thing."

"Are you serious?" Jessica demanded. "Liz, this is obviously the biggest social event of the season out here! Everyone in town will be going. Not to mention the guys who come *with* the carnival," she added, putting on a pair of over-size silver earrings. "I read a great book once about a girl who fell in love with a Ferris wheel operator. It was incredibly romantic. He was strong, but at the same time—"

"I know, I know," Elizabeth said, interrupting her. "Strong, but gentle." She couldn't help teasing Jessica when she got that starry-eyed expression on her face. "Well, somehow I can't imagine your meeting the man of your dreams at a carnival, Jess." She giggled. "And if you *do* find him there, don't you think he's going to be a little frightened by your outfit? He might think you're a lion tamer or something."

Jessica glared at her. "You just don't know

44

anything about fashion, Liz," she snapped. "Besides—"

Jessica never got to finish her sentence. A knock at the door signaled their aunt's entrance, which occurred, as usual, before either of the twins could say, "Come in."

"Dressed already?" Mrs. Walker said. She, too, was ready, her flowered dress complemented with matching pumps and a small handbag. She smiled approvingly at Elizabeth's skirt and sweater and then turned to look Jessica over, the smile dying on her face as her blue eyes ran over Jessica's outfit.

"Uh—Jessica, dear, don't you think you should—uh, aren't you going to change before we go out?" She managed weakly.

Elizabeth muffled a snort of laughter behind her hand, trying to make it sound like a cough. Jessica gave her a dirty look. "I *am* ready, Aunt Shirley," she said as sweetly as she could.

"Oh, dear," Mrs. Walker sank down on the edge of her bed. "Jessica, are you really sure you want to wear that to the carnival? Doesn't it seem a little—you know, a little—"

Jessica got a look on her face that Elizabeth recognized instantly as a danger signal. "I bought this jumpsuit especially for this trip," she

45

said sulkily. "I thought you'd really like it, Aunt Shirley."

"Well," Mrs. Walker said unhappily, "in that case—"

"Of course, if you really think it doesn't look good on me," Jessica added quickly, "I mean, if you really think that I'll *embarrass* you or something—"

"Of course you won't embarrass me!" Mrs. Walker exclaimed, flushing deeply. "It's just— well, you girls know how small towns are. People are accustomed to one kind of behavior, one kind of dressing." She fiddled shyly with her handbag. "You know, your uncle and I haven't had very much experience with teenage girls. I hope you won't take offense at what I'm about to say, but I know you are still a bit unfamiliar with . . . you know, with the rules of propriety around Walkersville."

"What are you trying to say, Aunt Shirley?" Elizabeth asked gently, putting her hand on her aunt's shoulder.

"Well, it's just that we have an unspoken rule in town about the carnival," Mrs. Walker continued. "The boys who work at the carnival are known as 'carnies' in local slang. Generally they come from very different backgrounds than

46

any of the boys in town. They're not necessarily *rough* or anything, but they're certainly not the kind of boys either of you two would be interested in. I'm sure you know what I mean," she concluded, getting up from the bed with an expression of immense relief on her face.

Elizabeth nodded, giving Jessica a silencing look. "Of course we understand," she said gently. "Every town has its customs, and we'd never do anything to act out while we're here, Aunt Shirley. You and Uncle Herman have been so nice to us."

"Thank you, girls," Mrs. Walker said faintly, stepping out of the room and closing the door behind her. Jessica, her eyes blazing, made a terrible face at the back of the door.

"Jess, cut it out," Elizabeth hissed. She glared at her sister's outfit. "I told you that wasn't appropriate! Don't you remember what Mom made us promise?"

Jessica stomped over to her dresser, grabbed a strand of big silver beads, and looped them around her neck. "There's no way I'm changing out of this now," she hissed. "Liz, I've got to tell you, I've had it with Aunt Shirley! She's treating us like we're seven years old! Aren't

47

we old enough to figure out who's good for us and who isn't?''

"Keep your voice down, Jess," Elizabeth said. "She'll hear you."

"And another thing," Jessica said, fuming. "Why can't we ever go anywhere by ourselves? Why do we always have to have Aunt Shirley and Uncle Herman tagging along with us? I don't know about you," she concluded, "but if I don't get out on my own soon, I'm going to— I don't know *what* I'm going to do!"

Elizabeth sighed. "They can't help the way they are, Jess. And we promised Mom we'd be patient."

Jessica's eyes flashed. "Well, I've just about had it with being patient. I don't think I can stand it anymore. This is our spring vacation and I want to start having *fun*!"

Elizabeth sighed heavily. She had been dreading that moment since they had arrived in Kansas.

She knew there was no holding Jessica back once she had decided she had had enough. And it looked as though that moment was here at last.

*   *   *

"You see, it really isn't a big carnival at all," Mr. Walker pointed out as they strolled from the spot where they had parked the car to the entrance of the municipal parking lot, where the carnival had been set up. Welcome to the Carnival at Walkersville! the entrance banner read. The twins glanced around them, disappointed that their uncle was right. It wasn't a very big carnival. A Ferris wheel was set up in the middle, but that, and a few other ordinary-looking rides, seemed to be it as far as the main part of the fair was concerned. Brightly colored tents lined the lot on both sides, and there seemed to be an abundance of food for sale as well as games to play. The twins strolled up and down with their aunt and uncle, making halfhearted attempts to win stuffed animals. Jessica seemed disappointed. "This isn't any fun," she said to Elizabeth after she had lost for the third time at ringtoss. "Let's get away and go explore on our own," she added in a whisper.

"Aunt Shirley? Uncle Herman? We're going to take a ride on the Ferris wheel," Elizabeth said cheerfully. Their aunt and uncle, engaged in a discussion with two elderly people near the ringtoss booth, waved the twins on with vague smiles.

"Horray—free at last!" Jessica exclaimed, hurrying outside with Elizabeth behind her. It was just beginning to get dark, and little lightbulbs dangling from wires were lit up around the booths and tents. Elizabeth's eyes shone. It was a beautiful evening.

"So, you want to go on the Ferris wheel?" she asked her sister.

Jessica laughed. "What better way to scoop out the action?" she said, getting in line for tickets.

Jessica was right. Minutes later they were looking out over the fairground. The prairie was so flat and open around them that the twins felt they could see forever.

When the ride was almost over, Jessica noticed a couple, three seats ahead of them. "Look. There's Annie Sue and Dennis!" Jessica exclaimed, she called their names, and when they turned, she waved energetically. Dennis waved back and smiled, but Annie Sue glared at them.

"That girl sure hates us," Elizabeth whispered to her sister. "I wonder why."

But Jessica wasn't paying attention any longer. She was staring, entranced, at a makeshift corral at the end of the fairground. "Liz," she said, grabbing her sister by the arm. "Look over there. Do you see what I see?"

Elizabeth stared. "You mean the horses?" she asked, squinting at the little corral.

"In front of the horses," Jessica said, her voice high with excitement. "See the guy with the riding crop? The one with dark hair?"

The Ferris wheel was slowing down now to let people off, and Elizabeth lost her view of the corral. "I didn't really get a good look at him," she said. "Why?"

"Come with me," Jessica said tersely as the man opened the safety bar on their seat. "I think we should introduce ourselves, Liz. He's the best-looking guy I've seen since we landed in Kansas! And if he looks half as good from up close as he did from the top of the Ferris wheel, I want to be the first one to get to know him!"

Elizabeth felt a warning bell go off in her head. She had seen that look on her sister's face before, and she knew it meant trouble. But she couldn't help feeling curious. And she wasn't far behind as Jessica led the way to the corral.

A few minutes later Jessica and Elizabeth were hanging over the corral, watching the dark-haired boy lead a little girl around the ring on a pony. Elizabeth had to admit the boy was unusually handsome. He was very tall, with broad shoulders and an excellent build. He had dark, curly hair and was quite tanned, with eyes that were an astonishingly beautiful shade of blue. He looked eighteen or nineteen. He kept looking at the twins as he led the pony in circles, and when he had helped the girl dismount he strolled over to where they were standing, an inquisitive smile on his face.

"You girls interested in horses?" he asked them.

"Oh, I love horses!" Jessica cried. "I always have," she added untruthfully, ignoring the incredulous expression on Elizabeth's face. Elizabeth fought the urge to laugh. The truth was that she herself was the twin who had always loved horses. She had gone through a phase in the sixth grade when all she cared about was riding. Still, it wasn't unlike Jessica to spontaneously develop a hobby, especially when it helped her win the admiration of a new boy.

"My name is Alex," the boy said, putting his hand out and shaking first Jessica's hand then Elizabeth's hand. "Alex Parker. My dad owns this carnival, and I'm helping him out by taking care of the horses during my spring break from college." He smiled at the twins, looking from one to the other with great interest. "I didn't know there were two such great-looking look-alikes in Walkersville," he teased them.

"Oh, we're not from Walkersville," Jessica said. "We're from Sweet Valley." Within seconds she was telling Alex about California. Elizabeth hung back a little, watching Alex with admiration. She couldn't believe it, but for the first time, she could understand why Jessica found a guy appealing. Usually Jessica liked guys Elizabeth would never consider dating in a million years. But this guy was really cute, Elizabeth thought. His smile was so nice, and she loved the expression in his eyes. He seemed smart, too. Not at all like a "carnie." She managed to cut into their conversation long enough to find out he was studying agriculture and economics at a college in Kansas City. When he asked her what her favorite subject was, she reddened slightly.

"English," she said promptly.

"Liz wants to be a writer," Jessica said. "She's really good, too."

Alex looked from one twin to the other, then smiled. "That's funny," he said. "You'd have a lot in common with my brother. He's majoring in English. He wants to be a journalist!"

Elizabeth raised her eyebrows. "You have a brother?" she asked. *I bet he doesn't look like you, though,* she couldn't help thinking.

As if he were reading her mind, Alex said, "I sure do. In fact the two of us have a lot in common with the two of you. That's why I was staring at you two before I came over to say hello. See, Brad and I are identical twins, too."

Jessica and Elizabeth stared at each other. "What?" they both cried. "You really have a twin?" Jessica asked.

"Hey," Elizabeth said in a low voice. "Looks like trouble is heading our way."

Jessica looked up and frowned as she saw Annie Sue come strolling toward the corral, her arm linked possessively with Dennis's. "Yuck," Jessica whispered under her breath. Annie Sue was about the last person she wanted barging into their conversation just then.

But she wasn't going to let the local girl spoil her sudden high spirits. Alex Parker was all she needed to turn Dullsville into Blissville, she decided. And whatever happened, she wasn't going to spoil her opportunity to get to know him better!

Five

Annie Sue came right up to the corral. She was dressed conservatively, as she had been each time the twins saw her. She was wearing chinos and a yellow sweater with a round lace collar that made her look younger than sixteen. "What beautiful horses!" she exclaimed, giving the twins a cold smile and then turning to Alex, her expression softening considerably. "Are you in charge of them?" she asked sweetly.

Alex nodded. From the look on his face, Jessica thought, he was sorry their conversation had been interrupted. Leave it to Annie Sue, she thought with disgust. Here they'd been on the verge of getting to know each other, and learning more about Alex's twin brother. Couldn't Annie Sue tell she wasn't welcome?

"I'm quite a rider myself," Annie Sue was saying, watching for Alex's reaction out of the corner of her eye. When no one said anything, she coughed gently and turned to Dennis for confirmation. "Aren't I, Dennis?"

"Yes," Dennis said, staring at the rhinestones on Jessica's jumpsuit. "Are those—excuse me," he mumbled, embarrassed, "but are those *diamonds*?"

Annie Sue didn't give Jessica a chance to answer. "Of course they're not!" she snapped. "They're fake, Dennis."

An uncomfortable silence followed. Jessica was trying to decide whether it would be better to let Annie Sue have it or try to seem cool and unruffled in front of Alex. He was *so* cute, she thought. She decided to let Annie Sue's comment pass.

"My name's Annie Sue," the girl told Alex, who smiled politely, introduced himself to her and Dennis, and tried to turn back to the twins to resume their conversation. But there was no stopping Annie Sue. She wanted to know all about Alex, his job, his association with the carnival, his courses at school, his interest in horses. She seemed fixated on the subject of horses, and when her lengthy description of her own expertise in the saddle didn't seem to hold anyone's attention, she proceeded to clamber up onto the fence, then leaned forward to pat the jet black stallion tethered by himself near the stable.

"Hey!" Alex cried, seeing what she was doing. He jumped over to hold the horse by its bridle. "Don't touch Midnight," he said sternly. "He's not completely broken yet. He's really not ready to be ridden or touched by a stranger." He patted the stallion soothingly. "Sorry," he added, smiling at Annie Sue. "I didn't mean to sound so fierce. It's just that I'm a little worried about Midnight. He's one of those high-strung, skittish beauties that's temperamental sometimes. And I guess I'm a little nervous about him because I'm the one who convinced my dad to stable him here this week. Midnight doesn't really belong with the carnival horses. He's a thoroughbred, and as I said, he's not totally trained yet. But I'm trying to sell him, and I thought the carnival might be a good place to attract attention for him."

"He's a beautiful horse," Annie Sue said appreciatively. "Do you think I could ride him sometime, Alex? If you were around to watch me?"

Alex shook his head emphatically. "I really can't let anyone ride Midnight. Sometimes he seems like he's OK, but the least little noise can set him off. Sorry, Annie Sue, but I'm afraid you'll have to stick to the other three."

Annie Sue looked disappointed. "Well," she said at last, "let's go, Dennis. Let's go see if we can find Mary and Hank."

The twins watched the brunette tug at Dennis's hand until he obligingly, though somewhat reluctantly, followed her back toward the game tents.

"I hope I didn't hurt her feelings," Alex said pleasantly, patting Midnight on the neck. The beautiful dark horse whinnied and tossed his neck feverishly before settling down again. "Shhh," Alex said several times, patting the stallion's velvety nose. "It's OK, boy. It's OK."

Elizabeth was staring at Midnight, fascinated. "I loved to ride when I was younger," she told Alex. "I can tell just by watching the way you handle Midnight that you have a real gift with horses." She laughed. "Some people have it, and some people don't. Right, Jess?"

Jessica gave her twin a murderous look. The fact that she had never been particularly horse-crazy was not something she wanted Alex to know about just then. "I think Midnight is gorgeous," she said. "Alex, I'd love to learn more about horses. Do you think you could . . ." She coughed, squirming under her sister's amused stare. "Do you think you could possibly find time to give me a lesson, or are you too busy?"

Alex's eyes brightened. "I'd love to," he said enthusiastically. "The only thing is that I'm really in charge here every night from five until ten." He was quiet for a minute, thinking. "Maybe you could meet me tonight when the carnival closes up. I could really concentrate then and not have to worry about anything else."

Jessica looked enraptured. "That sounds perfect," she said.

Elizabeth poked her in the side. "Aren't you forgetting something?" she hissed.

"What?" Jessica demanded, irritated.

"Alex, will you excuse us for just one second?" Elizabeth asked, moving away from the corral.

"Sure," he said matter-of-factly, walking the skittish black stallion back to the stables that had been erected alongside the corral.

"Liz, what on earth—" Jessica began.

"Aunt Shirley and Uncle Herman," Elizabeth

reminded her. "They're never going to let you come back here! Especially not alone. Remember what they said about being inside every night by ten o'clock?"

Jessica frowned. "They can't really be serious about that," she objected. "*No one* has to be home at that hour. Not even in Walkersville!"

"I don't think they were kidding," Elizabeth said. "Jess, you know how they are. They take things like this incredibly seriously. They're not used to teenagers. It isn't like with Mom and Dad! We can't argue with them!"

Jessica looked pale. "We'll have a serious, civilized discussion with them, then," she said. "Look, Lizzie, don't you realize what a great opportunity this is? This guy is *gorgeous!*"

Elizabeth sighed. "I still think you should think about Aunt Shirley and Uncle Herman, though," she objected. "At least don't make it definite with Alex. Don't promise to meet him before you talk it over with them.'"

Jessica looked closely at her sister. "You're not just saying this because you're mad at me for trying to get together with him, are you?" she asked slyly. "Is it my imagination, or do I detect the tiniest little bit of interest, Liz?"

Elizabeth blushed scarlet, hating herself. "I

think he's cute," she mumbled. "But so what? That doesn't make any difference."

"What about Jeffrey?" Jessica demanded.

Elizabeth drew a line in the dust with her toe. She had been wondering the exact same thing herself, but there was no point in letting her sister in on that. "What do you mean, 'What about Jeffrey?' " she repeated in a high voice. "I just said I thought Alex was cute, that's all." She gave Jessica a dirty look. "*I'm* not the one who tried to corral him—excuse the pun—into meeting me later on, am I?"

Jessica stared. "You really like him," she whispered. "Liz, I haven't heard you sound so defensive about a guy since you first fell for Jeffrey!"

Elizabeth could feel her face getting hotter and hotter. She couldn't believe how ridiculous she felt, standing there and bickering with Jessica about some guy they had met only half an hour earlier. But the truth was that she *was* attracted to Alex, and she felt more than a little guilty about it. For one thing, she wasn't used to being attracted to the same boy as her twin. It made her distinctly uncomfortable to realize they *both* liked Alex. Moreover, there was the question of Jeffrey. What if Jessica weren't around? Would she have tried to get to know Alex better?

Elizabeth shook her head, trying to clear her thoughts. "Listen," she said finally. "I feel silly even talking about this whole thing, Jess. I think you should do exactly what you want and leave me out of it. Just try to remember that we're guests at Five Elms. We don't want to do anything to hurt Aunt Shirley or Uncle Herman."

"Spoilsport," Jessica muttered under her breath, turning on her toe and heading back to the corral. Elizabeth sighed heavily, following her. Why did it seem so obvious to her that trouble was brewing ahead?

"Alex," Jessica said, looking up at him from under lowered lashes, "tell us more about your brother Brad. What's he like?"

Alex looked thoughtfully from Jessica to Elizabeth. "He's—well, he's a little quieter than I am," he said.

"Just like Liz!" Jessica exclaimed triumphantly.

"He's a better student than I am. Works harder in classes and stuff," Alex added.

Jessica poked Elizabeth meaningfully. "Like you!" she hissed as if Elizabeth weren't catching on to what she was trying to do.

"He's kind of an interesting guy," Alex continued thoughtfully. "He was born first, and he's always taken a sort of big brother attitude toward me." He looked down at the ground for a minute. "Our mom died when we were really little, and Brad . . . well, he kind of took charge of things around the house. I guess I always looked up to him for a whole lot of reasons. He's a tremendous guy," he added. "I bet you'd both like him a lot."

"Where is he?" Jessica demanded. "Isn't he at the carnival?"

Alex shook his head. "Brad isn't really very interested in the carnival. See, it's different for me. I love everything about horses. It's one of the reasons I'm studying agriculture: I want to have a horse farm one day and maybe even become a professional trainer or horse breeder. But Brad's much more academic. He's coming down tomorrow from Kansas City, but we probably won't see each other much." He frowned. "He's going to be helping my dad with the office work, so he'll be working in the mornings, and I work afternoons and evenings."

"Oh," Jessica said, disappointed. "Because I was going to say it would be kind of fun if we could all do something together. The four of us." She giggled. "I bet we'd attract a lot of attention!"

Alex smiled, but he looked slightly uncomfortable. "It would be great to do something together, but as I said, our schedules are going to be different."

Jessica seemed to be thinking fast. "Isn't it weird how much Brad and Alex sound like the two of us?" she asked Elizabeth. "You and Brad sound like you have so much in common!"

Elizabeth couldn't help laughing. She wondered if Jessica had any idea how transparent she was sometimes! Especially if there just happened to be a guy involved. It was perfectly obvious that Jessica was trying to give her a hint. Brad *did* sound like an interesting guy, but Elizabeth didn't see that there was much chance she'd ever meet him.

But she hadn't counted on Jessica's persistance. "Think what a riot it would be, the four of us going out," she continued. "Liz, we've never gone out with twins before!" Her eyes shone with excitement. "Alex, there's got to be some time when you two can get together. Let's try to arrange it, OK?"

"OK!" Alex said, smiling at her. "I'm sure Brad would kick me if he thought I was trying to cheat him out of a chance to get to know you girls," he added, his blue eyes twinkling. "Meanwhile, are we on for a riding lesson tonight after the carnival?"

"We sure are!" Jessica exclaimed, ignoring the look Elizabeth gave her. "I'll meet you here at ten-thirty," she added happily. Her expression was the brightest it had been since the twins arrived in Walkersville.

But that, at least as far as Elizabeth was concerned, was part of the problem. She knew that the look Jessica had in her eyes could only mean one thing: Jessica was falling for Alex Parker. And something told Elizabeth that the peace and quiet they had enjoyed until that moment in Walkersville was about to end for good!

Six

"So you girls enjoyed the carnival?" Mrs. Walker asked with a smile. They were sitting in the Walkers' beautiful family room, drinking hot chocolate, something the twins had discovered was a nightly ritual with their aunt and uncle. "You didn't think it was too small?" their aunt added anxiously.

"We had a terrific time," Jessica assured her, her cheeks turning slightly pink as she recalled the events of that evening. She glanced up at the clock on the wall. Nine-thirty. How much longer were they going to sit around talking like this? Was she ever going to be able to escape?

"We saw you over by the corral talking to Annie Sue," Mrs. Walker said with satisfaction.

"I told you she'd warm up! Isn't she a wonderful girl?"

Elizabeth and Jessica exchanged glances. They had agreed to keep their feelings about Annie Sue Sawyer private, knowing the truth would only make their aunt uncomfortable. But Jessica didn't see the point of lying to her, whatever Elizabeth said. After all, Elizabeth was the one who was always big on being honest. "I don't think Annie Sue likes us very much, Aunt Shirley," she remarked, setting down her hot chocolate and shooting another desperate glance at the clock.

"Doesn't like you?" Mrs. Walker looked horrified. "Goodness, Jessica, what on earth gave you that idea?"

Jessica fiddled with the silver beads she was wearing. "Well, I don't know. She just doesn't seem very friendly. Does she, Liz?"

Elizabeth looked uncomfortably at her aunt. "Maybe she's just shy," she volunteered weakly.

Aunt Shirley looked upset. "I can't imagine Annie Sue not being friendly! Why, I've been talking about your visit for months! I told her all about you girls, how pretty you both are, how sophisticated, how smart, how—"

"Whoa!" Elizabeth said, putting her hands

up in the air and laughing. "No wonder Annie Sue's been less than a hundred percent over-joyed to get to know us! She must be sick of hearing how great we are by this point."

Mrs. Walker looked puzzled. "I was only tell-ing her the truth," she said. "As far as I'm concerned, you two are simply the most won-derful, the most—"

Elizabeth burst out laughing. "You happen to be the world's most wonderful aunt!" she ex-claimed. "Which is why you're such a good public relations agent." She smiled at Jessica. "Maybe all we have to do to get Annie Sue to warm up a little is to reveal a few of our short-comings, Jess. Once she sees we're not perfect after all, I'm sure she'll relax, and everything will be OK."

Jessica frowned. She didn't feel like talking about Annie Sue right then. What she wanted was to get ready to go out again and meet Alex. Her heart raced a little at the thought. She couldn't believe how lucky it was that she'd spotted him from the Ferris wheel. He was *so* gorgeous, and he seemed incredibly nice, too. She couldn't wait for a chance to spend some time with him alone.

"Well," she said as casually as possible, getting up from her chair, "I'm going to grab a sweater. I thought I'd take a walk back into town."

"What did you say, dear?" Mr. Walker asked, putting down his newspaper.

Jessica reddened slightly, avoiding Elizabeth's gaze. "I said I thought I'd just take a little walk into town," she murmured, dropping her eyes. Her aunt and uncle were staring at her as if she had just announced she intended to commit a felony.

"*Walk* into town? At this hour?" Mrs. Walker repeated, aghast. "Jessica, it's a quarter to ten!"

"I know," Jessica said. "Don't worry," she added, although she knew it was pointless since they already looked distraught. "I won't be out long. I just want to get a little air."

Mrs. Walker bit her lip and stared helplessly at her niece. Jessica could tell she didn't want to interfere, but the thought of letting one of the girls walk alone to town seemed to be too much for her. "Why do you want to go back to town?" she asked. "Couldn't you just wait until tomorrow, and then we'll all go?"

Jessica coughed. "Uh—no, not really. I mean, I really feel like taking a walk. *Now*."

"Well, why don't we all take a walk then?"

Mr. Walker boomed, getting to his feet. "A little night air might do us all some good."

Jessica stared at him, the color draining from her face. This was the last straw. She couldn't stand the thought of a group expedition at this point, and it seemed that the only thing she could do now was to try telling them the truth. "Actually, I was planning on going back to the carnival," she said, trying to ignore the agonized expression on her twin's face. "I met a nice guy there tonight, and I'm supposed to meet him when the carnival shuts down."

"You met—" Aunt Shirley turned white. "Herman," she said weakly, clutching her heart. "My pills—"

Mr. Walker jumped up and fished around in a little wooden box on the coffee table. "Here you go," he said, bringing her a glass of water and handing her a small white tablet. "Your aunt musn't be excited," he said sternly, looking at Jessica with disapproval. "Now, Jessica, what's this about meeting someone at the carnival?"

Jessica looked at her aunt with dismay. "He isn't—I mean, he's not a 'carnie,' Aunt Shirley. Honestly. He's a really nice guy. And we weren't going to do anything wrong. I was just going to walk up to the carnival and—"

"Jessica," Shirley Walker said, setting down her water glass, "there's simply no point in discussing it. I know your uncle and I must seem like old fuddy-duddies compared to your parents, but Walkersville isn't Sweet Valley. Certain things just aren't accepted here. For your own good I have to tell you that it's out of the question for you to go back to that carnival unescorted at this hour, in the pitch dark."

"OK," Jessica said quickly. "You're right, Aunt Shirley." She gave the most winning smile she could manage. "I feel terrible. I should've thought the whole thing through." Elizabeth was staring at her, but Jessica ignored her and continued. "Do you two forgive me? I was acting like a real flake. I should have realized what a dumb idea it was."

Mrs. Walker's eyes filled with tears. "What wonderful nieces I have," she said, clasping her hands. "Jessica, you're so mature. You've understood our point of view so quickly! I would've expected you to put up a fuss!"

"Of course not," Jessica said sweetly, avoiding Elizabeth's accusing gaze. "I guess I still have a lot to learn about Walkersville." She paused for a minute and then yawned loudly, pretending to look surprised at herself. "Good heavens," she said. "I am *so* tired all of a sudden."

"*Really*," Elizabeth said, her eyes narrowing suspiciously.

Jessica yawned again, much more dramatically this time, and she stretched like a cat. "Boy!" she exclaimed, patting her mouth. "I don't think I can stay awake a single second more. It must be all the fresh air out here or something."

"You see," her aunt said fondly. "You're far too sleepy to go out again, after all!"

"Yeah," Elizabeth said, "it sure seems to have come on suddenly, Jessica. Maybe you're getting that disease that makes you fall asleep without any warning."

Jessica glared at her. "I think I'd better just go straight to bed," she declared, getting to her feet and yawning again. She gave her aunt and uncle each a good-night kiss and wandered out of the room, Elizabeth following right behind her.

"Thanks a lot," Jessica hissed when they had closed their bedroom door behind them. "You really helped me a lot, Liz."

Elizabeth glared at her. "Well, what's the idea, Jess? First you practically give Aunt Shirley an attack, telling her about going back to the carnival. And then all of a sudden you're collapsing from fatigue." She rolled her eyes. "Some smooth transition!" she said sarcastically. "I can't believe how trusting they both are. Mom and Dad would've seen through that in a second!"

Jessica was already over at the dresser, digging frantically through her makeup case. "I've got to hurry," she mumbled, taking out a mascara and touching up her lashes. "I'm going to have to take the bike from the shed, or I'm never going to make it back to the carnival by ten-thirty."

Elizabeth put her hands on her hips. "Funny," she said, "but you don't sound tired anymore, Jess. In fact you suddenly seem to be charged with energy."

Jessica giggled. "You're so cute when you're mad, Liz. Has anyone ever told you that?"

Elizabeth shook her head in despair. However hard she tried, she could never stay angry at her sister. But Elizabeth tried to keep her expression stern. "Would you mind telling me exactly what you've got up your sleeve?" she asked.

Jessica grabbed a bottle of cologne from the dresser and sprayed herself liberally with it. "I'm going to sneak out!" she exclaimed as if it were the most obvious solution to the problem. "You don't want me upsetting Aunt Shirley and Uncle Herman, do you?" she added indignantly.

Still frowning, Elizabeth crossed her arms. "And you're telling me that sneaking out of here at ten o'clock at night isn't going to upset them?"

"Not if they don't find out," Jessica said sweetly, dipping her little finger into a pot of lip gloss and applying it. "There!" she exclaimed, spinning around to face her sister. "What do you think? If you were Alex Parker, would you consider falling madly in love with me?"

Elizabeth rolled her eyes. "Jess," she pleaded, "can't you possibly just forget Alex for tonight and explain to him tomorrow that you have a strict curfew and that your aunt and uncle—"

"Forget Alex? You mean break our date tonight?" Jessica's eyes were round with horror. "Liz, you've got to be kidding! I'd rather die!"

Elizabeth started pacing around the room. "So that means I'm going to have to cover for you if Aunt Shirley or Uncle Herman comes in looking for you," she pointed out. "In fact, I'm actually going to have to lie for you, right? Tell them you're under the bed or someting?"

"Try saying I'm in the bathroom." Jessica giggled. "I think they'll probably consider that a little more likely."

Elizabeth glared at her. "Jess," she said angrily, "you know how I feel about lying. I'm not one bit happy about your sneaking out of here."

Jessica stared at her twin as if she were trying to decide the best strategy for winning her over. "Lizzie, please," she said at last, obviously deciding it would be best to plead. "I just don't know what I'll do without your help. I can't possibly stand Alex up. I promise I'll never do this again, but just for tonight, Lizzie, *please!*"

Elizabeth began to relent. "How are you going to get out of here without their noticing?" she asked finally.

"Simple. I'll just slip out the back door. Just promise to leave it unlocked for me, OK? I'll be back early. I promise."

Elizabeth shook her head with a sigh. "I'm not really happy about this, Jess."

But Jessica was already grabbing her purse and slipping out into the hall. She checked both ways to make sure the coast was clear, then turned back to mouth, "See you soon" at Elizabeth, giving her a last little wave before sneaking into the kitchen and out the back door.

There was nothing Elizabeth could do to stop her. And much as she hated to be part of the whole thing, it looked as though she couldn't prevent it.

Now all she could do was keep her fingers crossed that neither her uncle nor aunt would want to see her sister for the next few hours!

"What a beautiful night," Jessica said huskily, standing close to Alex and watching admiringly as he guided Midnight out of his stable.

"It is a nice night," he said, smiling down at her. "A perfect night for a riding lesson."

Jessica flipped her hair off her shoulder. Actually, there were several other things she thought it was a nice night for—like cuddling up under the big oak tree near the stable and getting to know each other better. But if Alex was going to spend the next week taking care of these horses, she figured she had better learn something about them. "You're going to have to teach me everything," she said, putting her

77

hand on his arm and looking up at him imploringly. "I don't know the first thing about horses."

"Wait a minute, I thought you said you knew horses?"

"I said I love horses, but I don't know anything about them."

Alex laughed. "Well, you may be the best person to ride Midnight, then. If you don't know anything about horses, you haven't learned any bad habits. See, Midnight is almost entirely broken in."

"Now I'm the one not to understand. I thought you told Annie Sue he wasn't broken in and that no one could ride him."

"I didn't want her riding him. He's just got an incredibly sensitive mouth. If he's handled clumsily, he goes berserk."

Jessica frowned, looking up at the huge, jet black stallion. She gulped a little. "You really want me to ride Midnight?" she asked uncertainly. "Shouldn't I start out on one of the tamer ones?"

"I'll be right here, Jess. Besides, he's perfectly safe as long as he's handled properly. Come on. Let me show you how to mount."

The next hour was one of the most wonderful Jessica could remember. It was such a new experience to be on horseback, to sit astride the powerful stallion, to feel his mane twitching against her hand, to feel the soft cool breeze against her face as Midnight trotted around the corral. To her surprise, she found herself learning the rudiments very quickly. Soon she could mount and dismount herself. And to her utter disbelief she found Midnight obeying the slightest turn of the rein. He was a gorgeous horse, and Jessica felt proud that Alex had trusted her enough to let her ride him.

"Now if he ever starts to act up, the thing to do is to relax the reins so you're not pulling on his mouth, and pat him right here." Alex showed her a place on Midnight's neck. "I don't know why, but that seems to help settle him down. And, remember, relax the reins. Most people panic when their mount panics, and their natural reaction is to pull back on the reins. Make sure you don't do that!"

Jessica caught sight of the illuminated dial of Alex's watch and noticed that it was already eleven-thirty. She had better head back to Five Elms soon or Elizabeth would murder her. "I feel terrible, but I'm going to have to go soon," she said as Alex helped her dismount. It was such a funny feeling sliding down off the stallion. Already she could see why Alex loved the horse.

Alex's hands lingered a split second longer than necessary around her waist before releasing her. "Too bad," he said softly. "You're a good student, Jess. I enjoyed out little lesson."

Jessica put her hand on his arm. "Maybe we could do this again," she suggested. "I still don't know more than the basics . . ."

Alex's face brightened. "I'd love to help you again." He beamed. "The only problem is that I can't ever get off work until the carnival closes. Do you think you could meet me again at the same time?"

Jessica thought quickly. True, she had promised Elizabeth that that would be the only time she'd sneak out. But even Elizabeth would understand that this was a real emergency. "I think I can manage," she said softly. *For you,* she was thinking, *I'd manage anything. Absolutely anything.*

"Too bad about my schedule," Alex mused. "It's a shame I can't get out early tomorrow, or I could introduce my brother to your sister."

Jessica's face lit up. What a perfect idea! Elizabeth was bound to forgive her for sneaking out of the house again if Jessica could make her a peace offering—such as an introduction to Brad. "Can't we all meet here tomorrow? We could introduce Brad and Liz then," she suggested.

Alex thought this over carefully. "Unfortunately, I've got to try to line up some prospective buyers for Midnight, and I'm not sure when I'll be here, so tomorrow won't really work. Unless," he added quickly, seeing the downcast expression on her face, "I just *make* it my business to be here. Meet us tomorrow afternoon at three. We'll both be here. I'll take care of business after that. Then you and I can get together."

"Alex, you're wonderful!" Jessica exclaimed. She gave him an impulsive kiss on the cheek, her pulse quickening a little as her lips brushed his warm skin. She liked this guy a lot. In fact, more than a lot.

Suddenly Walkersville didn't seem like Dullsville. In fact, there wasn't another place on earth where Jessica would rather be just then.

And she could barely wait to get home and tell her twin the wonderful news about Brad!

Seven

Elizabeth leaned over Jessica's bed, shaking her twin lightly. "Hey," she exclaimed a minute later when there was no sign of movement from the heap under the covers, "don't you think Aunt Shirley and Uncle Herman are going to be curious about how any healthy sixteen-year-old can sleep from ten at night till ten in the morning?"

Jessica opened one eye, groaned, and put her pillow over her head. "Go away," she muttered. "Aren't we supposed to be catching up on rest and relaxation out here, anyway?"

"Yep," Elizabeth said, sitting down on the side of her sister's bed and giving it a vigorous bounce. "But today we're going to Walker's to help Uncle Herman, remember? Today is Monday, and we're supposed to work behind the soda counter. Uncle Herman says Mr. Campbell wants us there by eleven.''

Jessica groaned again and sat up in bed. "Why do we have to do that today?" she asked.

"I won't remind you whose bright idea it was in the first place," Elizabeth said dryly. "How was last night?" she asked, curious. "You must've come in really late. I didn't even hear you."

Jessica rubbed her eyes, stretching languidly. A smile crossed her face as memories of the night before came flooding back. "You're not going to believe this, Liz, but I think I'm in love."

Elizabeth clutched her heart, pretending to faint. "No!" she shrieked with mock surprise. "I never in a *million* years would've guessed that could ever happen to you, Jessica."

Jessica sniffed. She never knew exactly how to respond when Elizabeth teased her. She looked thoughtfully at her sister, decided to ignore her, and continued thinking aloud. "Alex is amazing. He's so sensitive, so thoughtful—"

"Strong," Elizabeth interrupted helpfully, "but gentle?"

Jessica took a swipe at Elizabeth with her

pillow. "I'm serious, Liz. You're not even pretending to be interested."

Elizabeth was instantly contrite. "I'm sorry," she said sincerely. "Now, tell me every last detail. Did he manage to get you anywhere near one of those horses?"

Jessica's eyes brightened. "Liz, you wouldn't have believed it in a million years, but I actually rode Midnight—you know, the black stallion Alex was warning Annie Sue about. And it was OK! I mean, I was actually able to control him. I really had fun."

Elizabeth laughed. "Alex really must be special if he converted you," she mused. "I sure didn't have much luck getting you interested in horses when we were little."

"Well, you know how it is," Jessica said vaguely, getting out of bed and wandering over to the little closet they were sharing. "Now that I'm older, these things are much more appealing. I't all just a question of—you know—*maturity*."

Elizabeth grinned. She couldn't help wondering if Jessica's newfound maturity had anything to do with the fact that Alex was a college guy.

"What do you think I should wear to work

behind the soda fountain?'' Jessica asked, holding up a purple cotton sweatshirt dress that just skimmed her knees. "How's this?"

"It looks fine," Elizabeth said automatically. A funny expression crossed her face when she saw her sister reach for a matching cotton headband. "You know, I could've sworn I saw Mary—you know, Annie Sue's friend—wearing her hair in a headband exactly like that yesterday," Elizabeth said thoughtfully. "I wonder where she got it? I didn't think anyone around here wore headbands."

"I never saw anyone wear one," Jessica said, twisting her hair up in hers. "No one but me!" She frowned. "I sure hope your eyes were playing tricks on you, Liz. The way those girls have treated us really makes me mad. I don't want to have anything in common with any of them!"

"Maybe working behind the counter today will give us a better chance to get to know some of them," Elizabeth suggested. "After all, Walker's *is* kind of the town hangout, especially around lunchtime."

"And it may be even more so with the carnival in town," Jessica said, looking thoughtfully at her sister. "Which reminds me, Liz, I did you a real favor last night."

"Oh, yeah? What is it?" Elizabeth asked curiously.

Jessica leaned close to the mirror, outlining her eyes with a purple eye crayon. "Well, Alex and I sort of got on to the subject of you and Brad, and how natural it seems for you two to get to know each other. Anyway, to make a long story short, Alex and Brad are going to be waiting for us at the corral at three o'clock." She smiled with satisfaction at her reflection. "I kind of forgot about working at Walker's today. But don't worry, Liz, I'll stay at the counter so you can go ahead and meet them. I know you wouldn't want to miss the chance for anything."

Elizabeth stared incredulously at her twin. "I can't believe you did that, Jess," she said, annoyed. "Couldn't you have waited to ask me if I was interested in meeting this guy? I mean, he's a total stranger!"

Jessica looked astonished. "I thought you'd be overjoyed. And he's not *really* a total stranger. After all, you've met Alex. And they're identical twins." She giggled. "At least you know what he looks like!"

Elizabeth wasn't amused. "I just don't like—"

She broke off when she saw the look on Jessica's face. "Never mind," she said. "I know you meant well, Jess. And who knows? Maybe Brad and I will turn out to become best friends."

"Or *more* than best friends!" Jessica exclaimed.

Elizabeth frowned. "I feel kind of peculiar about it, though, you know, with Jeffrey and everything." She thought for a minute. "I don't think I'd be overjoyed if Jeffrey were to go out and meet some really beautiful girl while I was away this week."

Jessica shook her head impatiently. "Come on, Liz. You're on vacation! And it's not like you're going to do anything wrong. You're just going to meet a nice guy." She patted her sister's arm affectionately. "I'm sure Jeffrey wouldn't object to that."

Elizabeth looked thoughtful. "I guess it can't hurt just to *meet* him," she said at last.

Jessica was right, she decided. They had come to Walkersville to learn as much as they could about life in a small midwestern town and to relax and to have fun. It really didn't seem that there was any harm in going along later that day to meet Alex's twin brother.

And who knows, she told herself. *Maybe we really will get to be friends!*

*　*　*

The soda fountain at Walker's was a simple counter with a long row of stools. It was set up at one end of the dime store. Only simple foods were available, hamburgers and hot dogs from the grill and a variety of ice creams from the freezer section. A young woman named Mindy was on the shift for which the twins had volunteered, and within minutes she had coached them in all aspects of behind-the-fountain tasks. Mindy felt so certain the twins knew what they were doing that she left them on their own while she went to run some errands for Mr. Campbell.

"This is a lot harder than it looks in the movies," Jessica muttered, leaning forward to scoop out vanilla ice cream from a huge barrel under the refrigerated counter. She and Elizabeth had been working for only an hour, and by then their arms were aching. "If this stuff weren't so cold, it wouldn't be half as hard to get out," Jessica complained. "Can't we sort of heat it up or something? I think I'm getting blisters."

"Quit complaining," Elizabeth hissed. "Mr. Campbell's coming over to check on us."

The twins were both wearing the regulation striped paper aprons and matching paper caps.

89

It seemed to them that the minute Mindy disappeared, hungry customers began hurrying in. At first the only customer was Dennis Stevens, who had a Coke, then left, but by twelve-thirty the regulars started coming in for lunch, and the twins had their hands full.

"The next time we want to experience real Walkersville life, let's not do it behind the soda fountain," Jessica moaned as she raced to the end of the counter with her order pad.

Elizabeth couldn't help but giggle at the helpless look on her sister's face. She knew the customers were getting a kick out of the temporary help. "You two sure look alike," one man at the end of the counter remarked.

"They're just lucky they don't take after their uncle. That's all I can say," another man said.

"How good are you at flipping burgers?" Elizabeth asked Jessica under her breath.

Jessica shrugged. "About as good as I am at any of this stuff. Not very. But I'll do it if you'll try to get some of this darned ice cream out."

"Uh-oh," Elizabeth said. "Looks like Dennis has brought the whole pack back with him."

The doors to Walker's had just swung open, and Dennis strolled in, grinning. Behind him

90

there were six or seven guys, staring at the scene behind the soda fountain.

"Just what we need—more business," Jessica whispered frantically. "Liz, these hamburgers are sticking to the stupid grill!"

"Turn them over!" Elizabeth hissed, snatching up her order pad. She couldn't wait until things slowed down a little. Jessica was right. This *was* real work!

Unfortunately Dennis wanted ice cream, and so did all his friends. The twins thought the lunch hour crush was never going to end. They were overjoyed when the crowd finally thinned out, leaving just the group of boys.

"What a team!" Hank exclaimed, lifting a spoonful of chocolate ice cream as if he were making a toast. The rest of the group applauded, and the twins, beginning to relax again, couldn't help laughing. Soon they were chatting with the group of boys as though they were old friends.

"Do you girls have dates yet for the square dance on Sunday night?" Dennis asked shyly.

"Square dance? I forgot all about it," Jessica said. An image popped into her mind of her dancing with Alex.

"You're kidding! The big square dance the

night the carnival leaves is the best," Hank told them. From the way he was staring at her, Jessica had the distinct impression that he was pleased that no one had asked her to the dance yet.

But Jessica's attention was diverted from the conversation. The door to Walker's swung open, and Annie Sue came hurrying in, an annoyed expression on her face. Her friend Mary was right behind her, with four other girls.

"I should've guessed you'd be here," Annie Sue said to Dennis, her voice strident.

Dennis frowned. "We're just having some ice cream, Annie Sue. Don't get all bent out of shape."

The twins stared at each other, uncomfortable.

"We heard the Walker twins were playing waitress for the day," Annie Sue went on, putting her hands on her hips and glaring at the twins. "Having fun, you two?"

Elizabeth gave Jessica a silencing look. "It's actually harder work than we expected," she said honestly, giving the girl a friendly smile. But Annie Sue clearly wasn't in any mood to be appeased.

"I guess you both think everything we do in Walkersville is stupid," Annie Sue said defensively. "We all know you think we're just a bunch of hicks. You don't have to pretend, you know."

"We don't think you're hicks at all," Jessica blurted out. "What in the world gave you that idea? We—"

"You do so," Mary interrupted. "Annie Sue told us how you two laughed at us the first day you came. And how you mimicked us and said how stupid our clothes are."

Jessica and Elizabeth exchanged amazed glances. "That just isn't true, Mary," Elizabeth protested. "We really want to get to know you. It's just—"

"Don't believe a word of it," Annie Sue cried, putting her hands over her ears and making a terrible face. "They're bound to say things like that now, when their uncle is just at the other end of the store. You should have heard the things they said to me," she told the attentive cluster of girls.

Jessica was outraged. "Annie Sue, you're lying to them!" she exclaimed.

That was clearly the wrong tactic. Annie Sue whirled on her heel, her face blazing with anger. "And," she went on to her group of friends, "they're trying to steal our boyfriends! Well, we're not going to put up with it, are we?" She spun back around to face the group of boys, her eyes flashing fire. "Are you guys coming with us?" she demanded.

Slowly, sheepishly, the boys got up from the counter, mumbling apologies to the twins, who watched the mass exodus with disbelief. "Wow," Jessica said when they had all vanished. "We should've called on Annie Sue an hour ago. She sure works wonders breaking up a crowd!"

"I just can't believe it," Elizabeth said, shaking her head. "She's obviously poisoned that whole group of girls. Do you really think they believe we want to steal their boyfriends from them?"

"It sure looks that way," Jessica said cheerfully. "Look, Liz, I know how sensitive you are, but I don't think there's a thing we can do about that girl. She's straight out of *The Wizard of Oz*." She giggled. "The Wicked Witch of the West!"

Elizabeth frowned and began wiping the counter with a damp rag. "But I can't stand the thought of her telling lies about us. If only—"

"I think you should forget about it for now," Jessica interrupted. "Especially since it's almost two-thirty." Her eyes twinkled. "And I don't know if you've managed to let it slip your mind, but don't you have a date with a handsome identical twin at three?"

Elizabeth laughed. "I guess you've got a point," she said, slipping off her apron. "Let me go tell Mr. Campbell that I'm going," she said, taking off the paper hat and running her fingers through her hair.

Jessica was right. Worrying about Annie Sue and her friends was just going to have to wait.

Elizabeth smoothed her hair back with one hand as she approached the corral. To her surprise, Alex was alone at the gate. He smiled inquisitively at her. She couldn't help feeling a little disappointed. Why hadn't Brad been able to come?

"Hi, Alex," she said with a smile. "Where's Brad?"

He laughed, showing even white teeth. "*I'm* Brad," he explained, extending his hand. "Which one are you?"

"Elizabeth. Jessica forgot that she had to work at our uncle's store this afternoon, so she couldn't come."

"That's too bad," said Brad. "Alex had to

make arrangements to have Midnight trailed—you know, taken in a trailer to a prospective buyer's. He sends along his apologies and asked me if I'd come anyway." He smiled. "Our schedules are totally opposite, and he was afraid we'd never get a chance to get together otherwise."

Elizabeth smiled back. "You two sure do look alike," she observed. She blushed and glanced away. "What a dumb thing for a twin to say, right? People are always saying that to Jessica and me, and I've always thought it sounded pretty silly."

"Well, you're right," Brad said, resting his arms against the gate of the corral. "We *do* look alike." He thought for a moment, then chuckled. "Though we sure don't *act* alike. The course I'm taking in psychology now at school says that's called compensation. You make up for similarities in appearance by reinforcing differences in character."

"Really? That's exactly like Jessica and me!" Elizabeth exclaimed. "It isn't easy being a twin sometimes, is it?"

"It isn't," Brad agreed with a smile.

Elizabeth felt right away as if they had a special bond. When Brad suggested they take a walk together Elizabeth agreed delightedly. He was such a nice person, so relaxed, so thoughtful. It was especially pleasant strolling through the wide-laned streets out to the edge of town. Soon they were walking along the edge of a large dairy farm, and Brad, squinting at the cattle, predicted it would rain soon. "You can always tell when cows lie down that it's going to rain," he said with a smile.

Elizabeth couldn't believe how easy he was to talk to. When he said "Tell me about yourself," she found herself wanting to. And he proved to be a good listener as well. She told him all about Sweet Valley, her ambition to become a writer, her favorite hobbies.

"I love writing, too," Brad said. "I don't usually admit this to people, but I write poetry. Sometimes—" His voice broke off, and Elizabeth stared at him, waiting for him to continue. "Sometimes I think I'll be able to capture how beautiful this country is in poetry, but I know that I've never gotten close," he murmured.

Elizabeth nodded gravely. "I feel that way, too," she said softly. Brad's eyes fastened on hers, and she could feel herself reddening. He was so good-looking—and so different from his brother! He seemed much shyer, much more withdrawn. And so much more sensitive.

Elizabeth found herself wishing they could see each other again. As if he were reading her thoughts, Brad cleared his throat. "It's really nice talking to you," he said finally. "I don't often meet girls who like to talk about writing. Just my luck, though," he added, shaking his head with a smile. "How much longer are you going to be in Walkersville?"

"We don't leave till early next Monday morning—a week from today," Elizabeth said.

Brad brightened a little. "Maybe we could get together again," he said hopefully. Then his expression fell. "Only I can't really. I promised my dad I'd take care of Evie—that's our little sister—while he and Alex are at the carnival. So I really can't go out in the evenings."

"That's OK," Elizabeth said hastily. "My aunt and uncle won't let us go out very late anyway." She couldn't help feeling relieved that their meetings would be confined to the afternoons. Considering how much she liked Brad already, it would simplify her life if their dates took place only during the day. *Much less romantic*, she told herself.

As they walked back to the carnival together, they agreed to meet again the next day at three o'clock in front of Walker's. Elizabeth knew the hours were going to drag until she saw him again. Brad leaned over to kiss her cheek, and there was no denying that her pulse went a whole lot faster when he was near her!

For once Elizabeth didn't try to analyze her feelings. She just enjoyed the floating sensation as she went back to Five Elms. She knew one thing. She was glad she had agreed to meet Brad Parker! Walkersville looked very different all of a sudden.

And she was very, very glad that she was there.

"Girls!" Mrs. Walker exclaimed, coming into the family room. She had a big smile on her face. "You'll never guess who that was on the phone!"

The twins glanced up from the TV movie they were watching.

But Shirley Walker didn't give them a chance to guess. "It was Annie Sue's grandmother, inviting you out to her farm for the day tomorrow." She beamed and clasped her hands together. "She's arranged a special welcome-to-Walkersville lunch for you girls. Annie Sue will be there, and all her girlfriends. Now isn't that sweet? I told you Annie Sue really means well."

Jessica and Elizabeth stared at each other. A whole day at the Sawyers' farm? From the blank look on Elizabeth's face, Jessica knew her twin was as disturbed by the proposition as she was.

Who knew what mischief Annie Sue could cause in an entire day! It made Jessica's head throb just thinking about it.

But it was obvious there was no getting out of the invitation. Their aunt had clearly accepted for them.

"I wish there were some way out of it," Jessica muttered to her twin later in their bedroom.

Elizabeth frowned. "I promised Brad I'd meet him tomorrow at three. Do you think we'll be back in time?"

"Hey," Jessica said, intrigued. "You didn't mention making a second date. This sounds pretty serious to me. So is he really a nice guy? What's he like? Is he as cute as Alex?"

"He looks exactly like Alex. They're twins, remember?" Elizabeth said dryly. She smiled. "And, yes, he's a really nice guy. I have to admit I'm looking forward to seeing him tomorrow."

"I know how you feel. I can't wait to see

Alex at the carnival tonight," Jessica said, looking thrilled. The twins were planning to make trips to the carnival as many nights as possible, though they knew they would have to be chaperoned by their aunt and uncle, and would have to come back with them before it got too late.

But Jessica had no intention of letting her aunt and uncle's rigid rules spoil her fun. It was just a question of working out a scheme and sticking to it. The rest would fall into place!

Eight

Bright and early the next morning the twins were up and dressed in clothes suitable for a day on a farm—blue jeans, bandannas, T-shirts, and sweaters. Their uncle drove them to the Sawyers' farm, which was a twenty-minute drive from Five Elms.

"I can't remember spending a day on a farm before," Elizabeth remarked, trying to sound enthusiastic enough for both of them.

Jessica was slumped in the backseat. Clearly there were things she would rather be doing than driving out to what seemed to be the middle of nowhere for a day cooped up with the terrible Annie Sue. Both girls were already accustomed to the routine they had fallen into from their very first day at Five Elms, sleeping late, having long, leisurely breakfasts, and spending the afternoon exploring Walkersville, taking long bike rides, playing with the kittens, and relaxing on the big screened porch, going through old fashioned magazines their aunt had saved from the fifties. Jessica would have preferred another lazy day to what lay before them at the Sawyers' farm.

"It sounds like Mrs. Sawyer has arranged a fun day for you girls," their uncle Herman said as he drove. "I understand she's invited a whole group of girls out to have lunch with you. That should really give you a chance to get to know Annie Sue and her friends."

The twins exchanged glances. "Yes," Elizabeth said noncommittally. "That should be really nice, Uncle Herman." Actually she couldn't picture the lunch at all. Would Annie Sue dare to be as cold to the twins as she had been thus far? It didn't seem possible somehow, not in front of her grandmother. But it was equally hard to imagine the girl being friendly.

"Here we are!" their uncle exclaimed a few minutes later, turning off the main road onto a small gravel one marked by a white sign that read Sawyer. They drove down the gravel road for almost a mile before the twins caught sight of the farmhouse, an old-fashioned white clapboard one. It was fronted by wide fields. A tractor was parked near the red-painted barn and silo. The whole place looked exactly like a picture-book image of the perfect farm. The Sawyers' property seemed to be fenced off, but it was so large that it was impossible to see how far back it extended.

"It's so pretty," Elizabeth said, delighted. Even Jessica looked pleased as they climbed out of the car and strolled up to the farmhouse.

Mrs. Sawyer proved to be a soft-spoken, comfortable-looking woman in her early sixties. Her hair was a lovely shade of silver, drawn softly back from her face and coiled in a bun. Her eyes were a beautiful shade of hazel. She was wearing a cotton flowered dress with an apron tied over it, and she had flour on her face and hands, which she brushed off before hugging the twins. "You'll have to forgive me," she said, giving them a big, welcoming smile. "I've been making an apple pie for our lunch party. I wanted you girls to get a taste of good, solid farm cooking—only now I'm afraid you've got flour on you instead!"

The twins laughed. Elizabeth caught Jessica's eye, wondering if her sister was thinking the same thing she was: How could this friendly, expansive woman possibly be Annie Sue's grandmother? She seemed so warm, so kind!

Mr. Walker exchanged a few pleasantries with Mrs. Sawyer before declaring it was time for him to get back to town. He had to get back to the store, and there was an important town council meeting later that morning.

'Fine, fine,'' Mrs. Sawyer said, making little shooing motions with her hands. "Go on back, Herman. The girls and I will be just fine on our own."

The twins thanked their uncle for the ride and promised to call when they were ready to leave. "Don't expect them before two," Mrs. Sawyer said. "This lunch I'm preparing is going to take a good couple of hours to eat!" After the twins had said goodbye to their uncle, Mrs. Sawyer gave them a tour of the farmhouse. "It was built in the nineteenth century," she explained, leading them through the cozy, sunfilled rooms. "This is Annie Sue's room when she stays over," she explained, showing them a small bedroom on the first floor.

"Where is Annie Sue?" Elizabeth asked casually.

"Oh, she's going to come out later with the

girls. She said they would be here around noon," Mrs. Sawyer replied. "But I know Annie Sue left explicit instructions with her little sister Janie, who's around here somewhere. Janie's supposed to give you a tour of the whole farm and show you everything while I'm getting lunch ready."

"Here I am, Grandma!" a mischievous little voice exclaimed. "I'm nine and a half," the girl announced, grabbing onto her grandmother's hand and staring up curiously at the twins. "How old are you?"

"Sixteen," the twins said.

Janie was a cute kid, her brown hair worn in two long braids and her face covered with tiny freckles. She had brown eyes and was wearing a red gingham dress that could have been straight out of a Laura Ingalls Wilder book. Elizabeth couldn't believe how friendly the Sawyers were being. Maybe the day wouldn't turn out to be a disaster after all!

"Janie, why don't you show the girls around?" Mrs. Sawyer said. "Did Annie Sue tell you where to take them?"

"Yep," Janie said, hopping backward down the hall on one foot. "Come with me!" she called to the twins. "Let's go out to the barn, and I'll show you how to milk the cows!"

Ten minutes later the twins were in the cool, musty-smelling barn, looking around with fascination.

"Let's milk Brownie," Janie said eagerly, grabbing a big brown-and-white jersey cow and backing it out of its stall. "Here, Jessica, why don't you try first," she suggested, getting a small wooden stool down from the wall and positioning it on the left side of the cow. "Just sit down and reach underneath for her udders," she instructed.

The Sawyers' cows had actually been milked first thing that morning, but Janie was determined to show the twins what farm chores were really like. What she neglected to tell the twins— as Annie Sue had instructed her not to—was that Brownie was a temperamental cow. She let only Mrs. Sawyer milk her, and she kicked like crazy if anyone tried to milk her from the left side.

Jessica wrinkled her nose. "You really want me to go first?" she asked squeamishly.

Janie burst into giggles. "Come on. It's simple," she urged. "Just sit down on the stool and make sure you squeeze hard enough. And aim for the pail," she added, sliding a metal pail under the cow, who was mooing anxiously.

Jessica frowned. "Well, it sounds easy enough," she said, crouching down and sitting experimentally on the stool. "I just reach under there and kind of grab her?" she asked.

Janie nodded, backing off, her brown eyes wide.

Jessica took a deep breath and reached under the cow. She was about to touch the udder when Elizabeth jumped forward and knocked her off the stool. "Watch out, Jess. She's about to kick you!" she shouted.

Janie ran forward to hold on to the cow and was patting her reassuringly on the nose. "It's OK, Brownie," she kept saying.

"What happened?" Jessica asked, getting to her feet and wiping the sawdust from the barn floor off her jeans.

Janie shrugged. "Guess Brownie's just a little temperamental today," she said.

"I think Jessica was on the wrong side," Elizabeth said suddenly. "Aren't cows generally milked from *that* side?" she asked, pointing to the cow's right side. She remembered reading about cows when she was younger, and she knew it made a difference.

Janie made a face. "That's just what stupid city people always think," she said, pouting.

Elizabeth raised her eyebrows. Suddenly Janie didn't seem so friendly anymore. Elizabeth couldn't help wondering if Annie Sue had briefed her even more carefully than Mrs. Sawyer suspected. In any case, Jessica had come incredibly close to getting kicked—and kicked hard—by this cow, whatever the reasons. Elizabeth vowed to be especially careful for the remainder of their tour.

"Watch out," she muttered to Jessica as they left the barn together. "I think our friend Annie Sue has got this kid programmed to torture us."

"I think you're right," Jessica said darkly.

Janie proved to be a real pain for the next hour or so. She tried to steer the twins into poison ivy and would have succeeded if Jessica hadn't recognized the leaves. Janie took them on a long walk in the woods at the edge of the Sawyer farm, then ran off and left them when they had no idea where they were, coming back only when they were so confused and upset they were close to tears. She made the twins help her feed the pigs, which were kept in a fenced-in yard near the barn, and burst out laughing when Elizabeth was almost stampeded.

110

By twelve o'clock both twins were tired, dirty, and upset, but both still in one piece.

"I want to strangle that little brat," Jessica hissed to Elizabeth as they followed her up the path to the back door of the farmhouse. "I'm not kidding! If I get a second alone with her—"

"Well, obviously Annie Sue's been with us in spirit this morning, if not in person," Elizabeth fumed. "I can't wait to let that girl have it at lunch."

"You're not the only one," Jessica muttered. "If it weren't for Mrs. Sawyer, I wouldn't even *stay* for this stupid lunch." Her eyes widened with horror. "Liz," she gasped, putting her hand on her sister's arm. "You don't suppose Mrs. Sawyer poisoned the apple pie or anything, do you?"

Elizabeth laughed. "I think you're getting paranoid," she said. "Janie and Annie Sue may have it in for us, but Mrs. Sawyer just wants us to have a good time."

"I hope you're right," Jessica said grimly. "I don't want to miss my date with Alex tonight because of food poisoning."

"You've got a date with Alex tonight?" Elizabeth asked as they followed Janie inside the farmhouse. She stared at her twin, taken aback.

111

"I thought you said last night that you weren't going to sneak out again! Which," Elizabeth added, "is what you said the night before."

"Shhh," Jessica warned her.

"Annie Sue? Is that you?" Mrs. Sawyer asked, coming out of the kitchen and frowning down at Janie. "Oh, it's you, sweetheart," she said, leaning down to rumple the little girls's bangs. "Did you show the twins around, honey? I was hoping your sister would be here by now. She was supposed to be here half an hour ago."

"We had a nice tour," Janie announced, twisting one of her braids around her finger. She looked challengingly at the twins. "Didn't we?" she asked.

"Your farm is beautiful," Jessica told Mrs. Sawyer weakly.

"Really beautiful," Elizabeth echoed. "Can we help you get lunch ready, Mrs. Sawyer?"

"No, thanks. You're sweet to offer, but everything's ready. All we need now is the girls." Mrs. Sawyer frowned at her watch. "This really isn't like Annie Sue," she said. "That girl's usually so prompt you can set your clock by her. I tried calling her at home, but there's no answer. I wonder—" She frowned again, shaking her head. "Well, something must've come up

112

to delay them. Why don't we all go out on the porch and have some nice cold lemonade while we're waiting?"

The twins agreed that there was nothing they'd like better. *At least Janie can't sabotage us out on the porch*, Elizabeth thought with relief. *We've got Mrs. Sawyer to protect us now!*

But the discomfort of their morning as farm-hands was beginning to be replaced by a new kind of agony, the humiliation of being stood up. The four of them sat on the porch, sipping lemonade, making small talk, and trying to pretend they weren't watching the clock.

"What time did they say they'd come?" Janie asked at last, squirming in her chair. It was twelve forty-five.

"They knew we were planning to eat at noon," Mrs. Sawyer said unhappily. "I just hope they're all right. If there's been some kind of accident—"

"Oh, there hasn't been an accident!" Janie exclaimed. The next minute she stuffed one of her braids in her mouth and looked embarrassed.

"Janie," Mrs. Sawyer said warningly, "do you know anything about where your sister and her friends are? If you do, and you're not telling us—"

"I don't know anything," Janie protested in a

high, whiny voice. "I'm only nine," she added as if that explained everything.

Mrs. Sawyer looked incredibly embarrassed. "I hate to say this, girls, but I think we should start without them. I don't want to keep you here all day, and at this point—since they're so late . . ."

The twins were mortified. It was obvious what had happened. Annie Sue and her friends had decided not to come. They had given Janie explicit instructions on methods of torture for the morning and then had decided to round their day off by not showing up for lunch. It seemed especially unfair to make poor Mrs. Sawyer suffer, though. The woman was obviously close to tears as she served lunch to Janie and the twins, trying to ignore the six empty place settings around them. No one was very hungry by this point, and it was all the twins could do to force themselves to sample her beautiful apple pie.

By one-thirty they were all too glum to put on a brave front. "Let me call your uncle and explain," Mrs. Sawyer said tersely. After she had called and asked him to come get the girls, she made an effort to excuse her granddaughter. "Something must have come up," she said lamely. "Annie Sue is the world's most sensitive, kindhearted, friendly thing. . . . She would never have done this in a million years unless there'd been some kind of emergency."

Neither twin answered.

"Honestly," Mrs. Sawyer said, twisting her hands together nervously, "I just don't know what can have gotten into her! Maybe one of the girls got sick," she said. "But then you'd think she would have *called*. . . ."

"Look, Mrs. Sawyer," Elizabeth said at last, unable to bear the woman's pain and embarrassment. "What matters to us is the effort you went to. We're both really touched. And we don't think you owe us any explanation or apology. We just want to thank you for all the trouble you took trying to make us welcome here."

"Yes," Jessica said. "I mean, it sure isn't *your* fault Annie Sue never showed."

Mrs. Sawyer shook her head sadly. "There must be some explanation," she murmured again. "There just has to be!"

The twins' aunt seemed to feel exactly the same way. She listened to the girls' description of Janie's and Annie Sue's behavior with surprise and confusion, and in the end declared that the twins must have been mistaken about why Annie Sue hadn't shown up. There was no way Annie Sue would behave so abominably on purpose.

"We think she just doesn't like us," Elizabeth said thoughtfully. "You know, maybe she feels threatened by us—unrealistic as we all know that is." She repeated what Annie Sue had said the day before in Walker's, accusing the twins of wanting to steal the town girls' boyfriends.

"Good heavens," Mrs. Walker said, upset. "That's terrible! I wonder . . ." She frowned. "I can't imagine Annie Sue saying something like that. I wonder what on earth has gotten into her? *Now* I wonder if she purposely didn't show up for lunch today after her poor grandmother spent the whole morning slaving away in the kitchen."

"What we want to know is what you think we ought to do about it," Elizabeth said. The three of them were sitting in the family room.

"I can't think what's best," their aunt murmured. "Unless—well, I guess you just have to go on trying to be friendly. I can't really think of any other—I mean, I could try talking to Annie Sue myself, but—"

"No," Jessica said, upset at the thought of her aunt having to interfere on their behalf. "We can work it out ourselves, don't you think, Liz?"

Elizabeth nodded. *Or not work it out,* she was thinking. By that point she had very little hope of resolving the problem with the town girls.

The prospect of getting to know Annie Sue and her friends seemed slim indeed.

"I can't believe you're doing this again, Jessica." Elizabeth sighed. "What am I supposed to do if Aunt Shirley comes in here? I'm not kidding. I don't think you should risk it a third time. I'm tired of covering for you."

Jessica had twisted her hair into a topknot and was winding ribbon around it that perfectly matched her cotton geometric-print top. "I can't figure out any other way to see Alex," she protested. "Look, Liz, I feel bad about sneaking around behind their backs, too. But I really can't see any alternative." She dabbed on a bit of lipstick. "*You* got to spend time with Brad again this afternoon, after all," she pointed out, "it's only fair I get some time alone with Alex tonight!"

Elizabeth looked thoughtfully at her twin's reflection. "I wish there were some way all four of us could go out," she mused. "It doesn't really seem fair somehow."

"I know what you mean," Jessica agreed. "It would be so much fun if the four of us could get together!"

"Hey," Elizabeth said, sitting up on the bed and snapping her fingers. "Why can't we all go to the big square dance this Sunday night? The carnival will be closing down, so Brad and Alex's dad should be able to stay home with his daughter, which means they both should be free!"

Jessica swung around, her eyes shining. "That's a terrific idea!" she exclaimed. "I'm going to ask Alex about it tonight." She rushed over to the bed to give Elizabeth a hug. "Our very first double date with twins!" she shrieked. "And such gorgeous twins, too."

Elizabeth giggled. "Brad and Alex aren't bad-looking, either," she said. The next minute they were both doubled up with laughter. The prospect of the square dance seemed much more exciting.

Who cared about Annie Sue and the hostile

treatment they had received from her and the local girls? The twins were going to have a great time. And the square dance was going to be a perfect opportunity to show those girls that the Wakefield twins could get along just fine without their assistance!

Nine

Shirley Walker put down the magazine she was reading and looked thoughtfully at Elizabeth as she came bounding into the family room. It was just before noon on Wednesday, and Elizabeth was supposed to meet Brad in an hour in front of Walker's. After their wonderful walk the day before Brad had agreed to meet her a couple of hours earlier that day. They didn't have definite plans, but the prospect of just seeing Brad again filled Elizabeth with pleasure.

"Hi, Aunt Shirley!" Elizabeth said warmly, coming over to give her aunt a kiss.

"Liz, I'm glad you're here. I was just thinking about you girls, and I wanted to ask you a question. Do you have a minute?"

"Of course!" Elizabeth exclaimed, plopping

down on the flowered upholstered sofa next to her aunt. "That's such a beautiful piece of embroidery," she added, pointing to the needlework lying beside her aunt on a footstool.

"I'm making it for your mother," her aunt confided with a smile. "Liz," she said, frowning, "I'm a little concerned about Jessica. Has she been feeling well lately?"

Elizabeth thought fast. "What do you mean?" she asked, stalling. She didn't blame her aunt for being concerned. Jessica was still in bed, catching up on her sleep after yet another late night. To their aunt, who innocently believed Jessica had turned in before ten the previous night, it must seem strange.

"Well, does she always get this tired at home? I know I keep telling you girls this, but your uncle and I really don't know that much about teenagers. But we didn't expect your sister to be going to bed so early every night." Mrs. Walker frowned again. "I'm just afraid she's bored here, that there isn't enough for her to do in Walkersville."

Elizabeth shook her head vehemently. "Oh, that isn't true at all, Aunt Shirley! I know for a fact that Jessica's having a wonderful time. We both are," she reassured her. *I'm going to kill*

Jess for putting me on the spot this way, she thought. *Poor Aunt Shirley!* She thought Jessica was so bored she was inventing excuses to go to bed early.

Mrs. Walker sighed. "But so much sleep," she mused. "Do you think it's normal? Your mother called last night after you girls had gone to bed—she just wanted to say hello—and she couldn't believe it when I said you were sleeping!"

I'll bet she couldn't, Elizabeth thought. Aloud she said, "Well, you know what they say about country air." That sounded more than a little lame, so in order not to face her aunt, Elizabeth pretended to scrutinize her aunt's embroidery. "Besides, we were both worn out when we arrived here, Aunt Shirley. Especially Jessica. She's had a hectic schedule the past few months, tons of cheerleading and a lot of sorority stuff to deal with. She was tired out by the time we got here, and then all this fresh air and riding bikes and everything. . . ." Elizabeth took a deep breath. She felt guilty lying to her aunt, but she couldn't let her aunt believe that she and Jessica were bored in Walkersville.

"Well, I feel much better if that's all it is," Shirley Walker said and smiled. "Now what are your plans for today?"

Elizabeth thought quickly. Should she tell her aunt about meeting Brad? She didn't see why not. Besides, one white lie was bad enough. She didn't want to keep fibbing to her. "I'm meeting a new friend in town," she said, smiling.

"Really?" Mrs. Walker's face brightened. "Annie Sue or one of her friends? I was sure she'd thaw sooner or later."

Elizabeth shook her head slowly. "No, not Annie Sue. It's a guy, actually. His name is Brad Parker. His father owns the carnival, as a matter of fact. He's just down here for a week. He's a freshman in college in Kansas City."

Mrs. Walker frowned. "Liz, I thought you and I understood each other about carnival boys." She looked distraught. "Your mother would never forgive me if she thought I was letting you girls run around with that kind of fellow!"

Elizabeth colored. "What kind? Brad's a perfectly nice guy," she protested. "Aunt Shirley, I know how you feel about protecting us. But Brad is really sweet. And he's in college and everything. He isn't even working at the carnival. His father owns it!"

Aunt Shirley shook her head, distressed. "Your uncle and I don't even know him," she pointed out. "Can't you bring him back to the house and give us a chance to meet him?"

Elizabeth sighed. She didn't know how to tell her aunt that inviting a guy over to meet your family was a big deal—that it wasn't the thing to do before you'd even gone on a first date! She barely knew Brad. How could she ask him over to meet her aunt and uncle? "It's really not a big thing," she said awkwardly. "You know there's a special boy I'm seeing back home, Jeffrey, the guy whose picture I showed you the night we got here. Honestly, Aunt Shirley, Brad Parker is just a friend. You know I'd never do anything inappropriate!"

Her aunt didn't look convinced. "Well . . ." she said slowly. "I guess since it's just an afternoon date and everything . . ."

Elizabeth glanced at her watch. "I think I'd better take one of the bikes, if that's all right," she said, giving her aunt another hug. "Listen, I promise I'll be back in time to help you make dinner, OK?"

Aunt Shirley sighed heavily. "Your poor mother," she commiserated. "It must be so hard raising two girls nowadays! No one can even figure out what the rules are, let alone how to follow them!"

Elizabeth smiled as she patted her aunt on the arm. *Thank heavens she hasn't found out about Jessica*, she thought as she hurried outside and wheeled one of the bicycles out of the shed. *If it's this hard for Aunt Shirley to accept the fact that I'm meeting Brad for the afternoon, just imagine what she'd do if she knew Jessica was sneaking out at night to meet Alex at the carnival grounds!*

However many times Jessica insisted that each night's stealthy trip to the carnival was an exception, it was obvious by now to Elizabeth that it had become a routine. Early every evening Jessica became amazingly sleepy, slipped off to her bedroom, and got ready for the real part of the evening. Elizabeth realized that she was going to have to tell Jessica that her nocturnal visits would have to end. They couldn't risk hurting their aunt and uncle. And from the discussion she had just had with her aunt, Elizabeth could see now that the risk her twin had been taking was far too great.

"That's strange," Elizabeth said out loud as she locked her bicycle in the bike rack next to the tiny library off Main Street. She had just seen Mary Hamilton and her friend Carol walk past. Mary had her hair in a pink cotton head-band similar to the one Jessica had worn the day before! Elizabeth wouldn't have thought twice about that kind of coincidence at home, but in Walkersville nobody seemed to wear head-bands. Not twisted up bandeau-fashion, anyway. Even stranger was the fact that Carol, a small, slightly plump redhead who ordinarily dressed in blue jeans and sweaters, was wearing a sweatshirt dress that looked very much like Jessica's purple one.

Elizabeth found it mystifying. As she strolled up Main Street toward Walker's, she wondered if Annie Sue's resentment of and anger at the twins might stem from her fear of losing control over the girls in town. It occurred to Elizabeth then that Annie Sue must hold a position of unrivaled power among her friends. She was clearly the leader of her group. A girl used to being in charge of her friends might be made uneasy by the arrival of outsiders. And their aunt, Elizabeth thought, hadn't made things any easier by telling everyone how wonderful her nieces were.

In any case, one thing was clear: the fact that Mary and Carol were wearing Jessica-style clothes meant that the twins' were attracting attention.

And not just negative attention, either. These girls must admire Jessica, at least enough to adapt some of her most trendy clothes.

Elizabeth made a mental note to tell her twin later what she had noticed. She wondered if Jessica would enjoy being imitated, or if it would bother her.

Brad was leaning against a tree in front of Walker's, his arms crossed and a friendly smile on his face as she approached. "Hi, there," he said when she came up to him. He reached out and grasped her hand, squeezing her fingers tightly in his own before releasing her.

"Hi," Elizabeth said softly, dropping her gaze. He was even better-looking than she remembered from the day before. His dark hair shone, and his eyes—what an amazing color! He was wearing gray chinos and a light blue cotton shirt that made his eyes look even bluer. She liked his style—and she liked the way he looked at her, too. It made her feel warm inside.

"You know, I didn't really have anything special planned for this afternoon," Brad said thoughtfully, looking down at her. "I thought I'd leave it up to you. We could take a walk around town, or maybe drive out into the prairie. I've got my father's car with me this afternoon. What do you feel like?"

Elizabeth thought. "Let's take a long walk," she said. "I never get a chance to roam prairie at home, that's for sure!"

"You got it," Brad said. "I know!" he exclaimed. "Let's drive out to Peterson Bluff and then hike around there. The bluff is the most beautiful place for miles around. Have your aunt and uncle told you about it?"

When Elizabeth shook her head, Brad told her about the grassless, wild tract of land where the wind had eroded the prairie to form a dropping-off point so that the prairie almost seemed to take a step down the hillside. "It's gorgeous," he assured her. "I love going out there."

"How do you know so much about Walkersville?" Elizabeth asked curiously.

"I don't, really. This is only the second time I've come here with the carnival. But the last time we were here I did quite a bit of exploring, and Peterson Bluff is actually fairly famous, especially if you're a hiker, like I am."

"You really like the outdoors, don't you?" Elizabeth asked.

Brad nodded seriously. "The feeling I get when I'm outside, walking by myself, can't be matched. I guess my brother feels that way when he's with horses. Especially with Midnight, the stallion he's so crazy about. I guess being outside makes me feel . . ." He looked around him, apparently at a loss for words. "I don't know. It reminds me of how big the world is. You know what I mean?"

Elizabeth nodded. She felt exhilarated as they got into Brad's car parked near Walker's, and drove out into the countryside. She couldn't believe how beautiful it was to see nothing but miles and miles of grassland. The sun was high overhead, and they drove in silence for a while, just watching the endless horizon.

"It's so strange," Elizabeth said slowly, "to be so far from the coast. I never thought about it before, but I guess I've spent my whole life near the edge of the country. Here"—she looked around, her eyes shining—"we're surrounded by land. Does that feel strange to you?"

Brad stopped the car and put his arm around her. "I guess I'm used to being landlocked. You know I've never even seen an ocean?"

Elizabeth stared. "What? Are you serious?"

"Absolutely," he said as they climbed out of the car. "I've spent my whole life in the Midwest. I've done some traveling with my dad. You know, the carnival and all. We've gone all through Kansas—I don't think there's a town in the state I haven't been to or at least driven through. But I haven't gotten much of a chance to travel anywhere else. I'd like to, though—one day," he said.

He took her hand and they walked quietly for a while. When they were deep in the prairie, and they could hear the wind rustle through the grass, Brad stopped short and pulled Elizabeth into his arms, gazing into her eyes. "When I look at you it's a little bit like seeing the ocean for the first time."

Elizabeth swallowed, holding her breath as she stared up at him.

"Your eyes," Brad whispered, brushing her hair back from her face. His hand was so gentle it felt almost as if it were the wind blowing her hair back. "Your eyes are just the color I always imagined the ocean to be. Sort of green and blue all at once."

Elizabeth pulled back, taking a deep breath. Suddenly she felt confused—and frightened. What she had felt just then, when he pushed her hair back from her forehead . . . the way his eyes fastened on hers . . .

For the first time in ages she forgot about Jeffrey. It made her feel peculiar. And she suddenly wondered if it would have been smarter to spend the afternoon wandering around town instead of coming all the way out to look at Peterson Bluff.

It took almost twenty minutes to cross the prairie to the bluff, and within that time they managed to steer their conversation back to less intimate topics. Elizabeth found Brad easy to talk to—about everything. He also shared her reverence for nature. And he had a good sense of humor and seemed to relish a chance to talk about growing up as a twin. Elizabeth was surprised more than once by his curiosity about Jessica—whom, she realized, he hadn't even met. He wanted to know as much about Jessica as he could find out—whether she had a boyfriend, whether she had ever been in love or had had her heart broken. Elizabeth found his interest strange, but at the same time she was relieved that the moment they had shared earlier had passed.

"You're a funny guy," Elizabeth observed as they approached the bluff.

"What do you mean?" Brad asked.

"I don't know. You just seem—" Elizabeth shook her head. "You almost seem like two different people. Sometimes you're serious and withdrawn. And sometimes you seem much more—I don't know—outgoing, almost brusque."

Brad shrugged and smiled. "I guess I am a little moody," he admitted. He didn't seem eager to pursue the subject. "Look, Liz, you can see the bluff from here!"

Sure enough, Peterson Bluff was worth the drive and long walk. The prairie did appear to drop off into midair, as if she and Brad had walked right to the edge of the earth. "Brad, it's gorgeous!" Elizabeth exclaimed, her eyes shining.

Suddenly Brad was staring at her again, with the same look in his eyes that had frightened her earlier. "So are you, you know that?" he murmured. She was certain then that he was going to kiss her. Her heart began to pound as he put his hands on her shoulders and faced her.

But he didn't kiss her. And she couldn't sort through her own feelings clearly enough to tell whether she was disappointed or relieved.

"Jeffrey called," Jessica informed her when Elizabeth walked into their room at four-thirty. Jessica was lying on her stomach on her bed, looking through the same issue of *Vogue* she had been reading for days.

"You're going to have that thing memorized," Elizabeth said, teasing her. She hung up her jacket and slipped out of the bedroom again, heading for the phone in the family room. She didn't feel like talking to her sister about the events of that afternoon. She was a little too unsettled about Brad Parker. What she wanted was to hear Jeffrey's voice, to tell him that she missed him, to hear what was happening at home.

Elizabeth used her parents' long distance calling number, so the call could be charged to her parents' phone. It seemed to take ages before Jeffrey came on the phone.

"Hey, it's me," Elizabeth said huskily.

"Liz! I'm so glad you called back," Jeffrey exclaimed. "Do you have any idea how much I miss you?"

Elizabeth felt her eyes fill with tears. Suddenly she missed Jeffrey too, so badly she couldn't believe it. She felt that she would do anything then to hold him in her arms.

"Tell me about your aunt and uncle. And are you guys behaving yourselves?" Jeffrey asked.

Elizabeth giggled. "More or less. I've got so

much to tell you," she began. Suddenly everything felt perfectly normal again. She began to fill him in on Annie Sue, the dreadful day at the farm, the charm of Walkersville, the carnival—even Jessica's adventures with Alex. The only thing she left out was Brad Parker and her walk that afternoon to Peterson Bluff.

"Where were you this afternoon? Jessica said you were 'somewhere,' " Jeffrey said.

Elizabeth twisted the phone cord around her finger. "I was just wandering around town," she said slowly. She fiddled with the telephone cord, wishing she could tell him everything that had happened. She was sure now that her attraction to Brad wasn't one bit important. It was so wonderful to hear Jeffrey's voice and to remember how much she loved him.

But she couldn't see what good it would do to tell him about Brad just then. It would only make him worry. That sort of thing was so much harder to talk about on the phone than in person. She would tell him all about it when she got back to Sweet Valley, and they would both laugh. She was sure of that now.

For now it was enough just to hear his voice again. And to say "I love you" to him and mean it—with all her heart.

Ten

Elizabeth had intended to get Jessica alone at the first opportunity to tell her about the talk she had had with their aunt that morning. But in her confusion about Brad, it had slipped her mind. Then she was busy talking with Jeffrey, and by the time she got off the phone, Jessica was in the kitchen with their aunt. She was leaning on the counter with both elbows and listening to stories about their mother when she was sixteen. With setting the table, making the salad, helping fry chicken and eating, there wasn't a second to get her sister alone. Elizabeth became increasingly upset as the evening wore on, and Jessica showed no sign of budging from her aunt and uncle's side. Elizabeth knew her twin intended to sneak out again that night, and she felt she had to do something to stop her. But what could she do as long as her aunt and uncle were within earshot?

At about nine o'clock Jessica's usual evening theatrics began. "Good heavens," she announced with an experimental yawn. "What *is* it about this climate that makes me so sleepy all the time?"

Mr. and Mrs. Walker exchanged concerned glances.

Jessica paused significantly, eyed the clock, and stretched, making as much noise as possible. "*My*, I'm tired," she declared.

"Jess, darling, it's only nine o'clock," her aunt pointed out.

"*Is* it?" Jessica asked with apparent shock. "I just don't know what's going on," she added, rubbing her eyes for effect. "Maybe it's being in a different time zone," she added. "I could have jet lag, you know."

"You've only moved two time zones, dear," her uncle reminded her. "And in any case you've been here almost a week now. You should be adjusted by now, even if you'd crossed the ocean."

"Oh," Jessica said, thinking that over. "Well, maybe I'm still growing," she suggested. "I read in a magazine that teenagers can hit little growth spurts and get really tired from them."

"We're just afraid you're coming down with something, dear," Mrs. Walker said. She turned to her husband. "I think we ought to call Dr. Bloomfield tomorrow," she said to her husband. "It doesn't seem normal for a healthy teenager to be so exhausted by nine o'clock every night."

Jessica yawned dramatically. "My," she said again, patting her mouth. "My, my, my. I really do feel like I'd better go to bed soon."

"Maybe you're not getting a good night's sleep in that little bedroom," Mrs. Walker said anxiously. "If you tried sleeping upstairs in a double bed, dear—"

Jessica looked alarmed. "Oh, I couldn't do that! I mean, I'm all settled downstairs. Besides, Liz would be really lonesome."

"Yeah," Elizabeth said dryly. "I'd be heartsick, Jess."

Jessica stood up and gave a pronounced yawn for good measure. "I'm going to go to bed now, everyone," she declared. "I promise I'm not sick or anything, Aunt Shirley. I'm just sleepy, that's all."

"Well, dear, if you say so." Mrs. Walker sighed as she watched Jessica leave the room.

"I think we ought to call Alice and Ned," Mr. Walker said, frowning. "It really doesn't seem healthy, Shirley. The girl shouldn't be so exhausted every night at this time. Not when she's sleeping as late as she's been sleeping."

"Uh—I think I'll just go check on Jessica," Elizabeth said, getting up from the sofa and hurrying out of the room. She closed the bedroom door firmly behind her and glared at her sister.

"Do you have any idea how much trouble we're about to get into?" Elizabeth demanded. "Aunt Shirley and Uncle Herman are talking about calling Mom and Dad!"

"Why?" Jessica asked, shaking out a pair of bright pink pants and stepping into them. "I can't believe how easily those two get upset. All I do is yawn, and they practically call the police."

"They're *worried* about you," Elizabeth seethed. "Poor Aunt Shirley thinks you're pretending to be sleepy because you're so bored here."

Jessica's eyebrows shot up. "Really? That's interesting." She smoothed the pants over her slim hips, admiring her reflection. "Maybe I should play along with that, Liz. Then they'd cool out on calling this Dr. Bloomfield tomorrow."

"Jess," Elizabeth cried. "Don't you see you can't possibly sneak out of here tonight? They're really worried about you, and probably a little suspicious by this point, too. Though God knows they're the world's most trusting people," she added. "Mom and Dad aren't, though. They're bound to figure out something weird is going on if they talk to Aunt Shirley again tonight."

"Again?" Jessica asked. "You mean they've already talked once?"

"Last night." Elizabeth moaned. "Mom called, and I'm sure Aunt Shirley filled her in on all the gory details. Jess, *please* stay in tonight. This is getting crazy."

"I can't," Jessica told her, slipping on her cowboy boots. "Alex promised to teach me how to canter on Midnight tonight." She gave Elizabeth a meaningful look. "Things are really getting somewhere between us," she added. "I have a feeling tonight's going to be a real turning point."

"Yeah," Elizabeth said morosely. "It sure will. Mom and Dad will probably be convinced you have mono or something and fly out here on the first plane they can get."

"Don't worry so much," Jessica chided. "I promise I'll be back early," she added, relenting when she saw the expression on Elizabeth's face. Before Elizabeth could make a further comment, Jessica had grabbed her purse and her jacket and slipped out the bedroom door. "Leave the door unlocked," she whispered. The next minute she was gone.

Elizabeth looked nervously at the clock. It was nine-thirty. She wasn't sleepy, but she was afraid if she went back out to the living room, her aunt and uncle would really think something weird was going on. She was pacing up and down the room, trying to figure out what to do, when she heard her aunt's characteristic knock on the door.

"Girls? Are you asleep yet?" Mrs. Walker inquired, opening the door—as always—without waiting for a response.

Elizabeth stared at her, terrified. Now what was she supposed to do? Her eyes flew around the room, looking for telltale clues that Jessica was gone. Then she looked over her aunt's shoulder. To Elizabeth's relief the door to the bathroom across the hall was closed.

"Where's Jessica?" Mrs. Walker asked, her blue eyes worried.

"Uh—she's in the bathroom," Elizabeth said. "Jess, hurry up in there!" she called. "She said she might be a little while," she added apologetically to her aunt. "She has about a million things she puts on her skin before she goes to bed," she added, improvising as fast as she could.

"Well, we decided not to call your mother and father," Mrs. Walker said, sitting down on the edge of the bed. Elizabeth stared at her. *Don't sit down*, she pleaded silently. *Don't look as if you plan on sitting there until Jessica comes out of the bathroom!* Things were going from bad to worse very quickly, and Elizabeth wasn't sure how much longer she'd be able to cover for her twin.

"We didn't want to worry them," her aunt added. "I guess things like this are fairly common with girls your age. It could be anything—a virus, the change in climate"—She cleared her throat—"even depression," she whispered meaningfully.

"True," Elizabeth said uneasily. "You know," she added suddenly, dropping her voice to a confidential whisper, "maybe Jess *is* a little depressed, Aunt Shirley. Do you think—I hate to ask you this—but if you left us alone, maybe I could get her to confide in me."

Aunt Shirley got up, her eyes brightening.

"Of course," she said. "How thoughtless of me! You're absolutely right, Liz. If she is a little depressed, it certainly won't help to have us hovering over her, asking her all sorts of questions."

"You're so understanding," Elizabeth whispered, feeling terrible. How could she do this to her poor aunt? She felt like a criminal as she led her aunt to the door, promising to report whatever she uncovered about her sister's distressed emotional state.

That was a close call, she thought, closing the bedroom door behind her aunt. She didn't know how much longer Jessica was going to be able to carry off her secret nighttime visits to the corral. But she did know one thing. She didn't want any part of covering for her twin anymore.

Jessica didn't know it yet, but she was about to lose her partner in crime!

"You really think I'm ready to canter?" Jessica asked eagerly. She was standing by the gate of the corral, looking with awe at the beautiful black stallion Alex was leading out from the stables.

"Sure," he said, giving her a smile and tousling her hair. "You and Midnight make a great team," he added. "You're one of the few people I've seen who he really responds to." Patting the horse's neck, Alex sighed. "It's a shame I have to sell him," he added sadly. "I wish there were some way I could afford to buy him from my dad myself—or at least stable him up in Kansas City for a while. I haven't found anyone who wants to buy him who I could bear to sell him to."

"I wish I could buy him," Jessica said impulsively. "He really is magnificent!"

"Come on," Alex said, grinning at her. "Let me give you a boost. Let's see you canter!"

The next hour passed in a blur for Jessica. Alex had saddled a horse for himself, and they rode out of the town and into the country. Jessica was exuberant. She loved the sense of power she experienced as she controlled the stallion. "Come on, Midnight," she whispered to him, pressing his sides gently with her knees. All it took was the slightest pressure, and he doubled his speed.

"You were wonderful!" Alex exclaimed when they got back to the corral. He helped her dismount, catching her around the waist. This time he didn't let go. She was between the horse and him, her hand still up on the pommel of the saddle. Alex was holding her with both arms. She turned, slipping her arms around his neck, and the next thing she knew his mouth was on hers. With one hand he held the back of her head as he kissed her, and with the other he steadied Midnight, who neighed restlessly while they kissed.

Jessica pulled away, breathless. "I think Midnight is jealous," she said, trying to seem calm. Her heart was pounding, and it was almost a relief to watch Alex lead the stallion back to the stable.

"I think we need to talk," Alex said softly after he returned from taking the horses' saddles and bridles off and covering them with blankets.

"Talk about what?" she murmured. He put his arm around her, and her heart began to pound again.

"About the fact"—he traced the outline of her jaw with his finger—"that I'm starting to fall in love with you, Jessica Wakefield."

Jessica stared at him, her lips quivering. "Alex—" she began. She felt that there were millions of things she wanted to say to him. That she was going to be there only until Sunday. That they barely knew each other. But talking wouldn't change the way she felt. And Jessica knew she was a little bit in love with Alex, too.

Everything about that evening had been magical. The chance to ride Midnight, the moonlight, the strength of Alex's arms as he pulled her close to him. Jessica put her arms around him again, closing her eyes as his lips came closer. Who cared how little time they had left?

Whatever happened—however hard it would be to say goodbye—it was worth it for the magic of that moment. She never wanted him to let her go. She never wanted the magic of his kiss to be over.

"Will you be able to meet me again tomorrow night?" Alex asked Jessica, helping her unlock her bicycle from the rack in front of the library.

Jessica frowned. "My aunt and uncle have been kind of worried about me. I think they're starting to get suspicious," she told him. "Isn't there any way we can get together during the day tomorrow instead?"

Alex was quiet for a minute or two, considering. "I don't think so," he said. "I have two or three people who want to look at Midnight, and then I've got to open the corral at three-thirty."

"OK," Jessica said impulsively. "Then I'll meet you here tomorrow night. Why don't I meet you around eight-thirty or nine? That way I can keep you company during the last part of your shift."

Alex nodded. "That sounds good. And I can get my dad's car and drive you home when the carnival closes down."

Her aunt and uncle would never let Alex drive her home, Jessica thought. But she'd worry about that later. She fiddled with her bike lock. "Oh, by the way, Alex. Were you planning on going to the square dance on Sunday night?"

Alex blinked, surprised. "Uh—not really. No, I wasn't. Why?"

"Because," Jessica said, stung. "I want you to *take* me, silly!"

Alex hesitated. "I told my father—"

"Alex Parker, it's our last night in Walkersville! If you come up with some flimsy excuse, I'm going to be furious." Jessica pouted at him. "Besides, Liz and I have already talked it over, and we decided we absolutely *have* to make it a double date. It isn't fair that the four of us haven't gotten a chance to get together."

Alex laughed. "OK, OK," he said, relenting. "It's a date."

Jessica squealed and threw her arms around his neck. "I knew you'd say yes," she said, delighted. "You're the most wonderful, the most fantastic, the nicest, sweetest, kindest guy who ever lived!"

"Hey," Alex said, his voice changing slightly. "That girl who's looking at us is familiar. Do we know her, the one over there in the red dress? She's staring at you like you just murdered her best friend."

Jessica dropped her arms and turned to follow his gaze. "Uh-oh," she said softly.

"What is it?" Alex asked.

"That's the girl who tried to talk to you about horses the night we met. And I think," Jessica said with a sigh, "my luck has just run out. Her name is Annie Sue Sawyer. Just believe me when I tell you that I think I'm about to be in for it."

"Why?" Alex asked, mystified.

"Because she hates me," Jessica told him. "Ever since I got to Walkersville she's done anything she could to make my life miserable.

And now that she's seen us together, I've just given her enough ammunition to make sure she succeeds!"

Annie Sue was standing about a dozen yards away, holding Dennis's hand and watching the scene before her intently. Jessica could tell from the expression on her face that the girl hadn't missed a thing. She had seen Jessica out after eleven—and with a "carnie."

Jessica knew she was in trouble now. All Annie Sue had to do was tell her aunt and uncle what she'd seen, and the twins' wonderful vacation would be destroyed. They would probably get sent home on the first plane, and their parents would never trust them again.

Jessica shivered. A wonderful evening had suddenly turned into a nightmare!

Eleven

"I don't see what good being mad at me is going to do," Jessica complained. She and Elizabeth were riding their bicycles into town. It was Thursday, and the twins had promised their uncle that they would go to Walker's and help behind the fountain again. It was a beautiful morning, but Elizabeth was in no mood to appreciate the scenery around them. She was still furious with Jessica for the position she had been put in the past few nights.

"It wasn't my fault," Jessica added, pedaling furiously to catch up with Elizabeth. "It wasn't like I knew Aunt Shirley was going to come back in, checking up on me or anything."

"Next time," Elizabeth fumed, "I'm not going to say a word. I'm just going to let her barge right into the bathroom and find out you're not in there. And you know what'll happen then?"

Jessica didn't answer. She was thinking uneasily about Annie Sue.

"They'll send us straight back to Sweet Valley," Elizabeth snapped. "And Mom and Dad will never let us take another trip alone as long as we live!"

Jessica bit her lip anxiously. "You really think they'd be that upset if they found out, Lizzie?"

"Of course they would be! Jess, don't be crazy! You know how Aunt Shirley and Uncle Herman are. Aunt Shirley practically had an anxiety attack when I went to meet Brad the other day—in the *afternoon*."

"Maybe you're right," Jessica said in a small voice.

"I hope last night was worth it," Elizabeth added bitterly.

"Oh, it was!" Jessica said, trying to shake the memory of Annie Sue's triumphant smirk. "Liz, I think I'm really in love with Alex. Seriously in love with him."

Elizabeth slowed down as they reached Main Street. "That's nice," she said absently. From her tone it was obvious she wasn't taking her twin's declaration seriously.

"You don't even care," Jessica said, hurt. "This may be the biggest thing that ever happens to me, Liz. Suppose I convince Mom and Dad to let me come out here and go to school in Walkersville, and live with Aunt Shirley and Uncle Herman, so I can see Alex more often. You probably wouldn't even care!"

"Somehow I don't see that happening," Elizabeth said dryly. "And, anyway, how would you manage to see Alex? You couldn't sneak out of the house and make it all the way to Kansas City." She giggled. "You'd have to start getting sleepy at about three o'clock in the afternoon every day!"

Jessica didn't look amused. "You'll be really sorry," she said, sniffing, as they got off their bikes and put them in the bike rack. "When Alex and I get married and open our own horse farm, you'll come begging to ride, and we won't even talk to you."

Elizabeth shook her head. "Jess, I think you're really losing it," she muttered. "Come on. We're supposed to be behind the counter already."

Jessica took a brand-new headband out of her bag and twisted up her hair, admiring her reflection in the shop fronts as they walked up

Main Street to Walker's. "Isn't this great?" she asked. "I bet I've got the only rhinestone-studded headband in town."

Elizabeth laughed. "That reminds me, Jess. I meant to tell you this yesterday, but—" She giggled again. "I guess you were too hard to get hold of between naps. Have you noticed that several girls around here are wearing the Jessica look the past day or two?"

"What do you mean?" Jessica asked.

"It's really weird. I saw Mary Hamilton wearing a pink headband, and her friend Carol had a dress on that was almost exactly like your purple sweatshirt dress."

"Hmmm," Jessica said. "Am I supposed to be flattered? Somehow the thought of Mary Hamilton or her friend Carol dressing like me doesn't thrill me."

The twins strolled into Walker's together, chatted with Mr. Campbell for several minutes, and slipped on the striped aprons. Jessica hated the cap that was part of the uniform and decided she wouldn't wear it unless Mr. Campbell insisted. The dime store was almost empty, and as it was still only midmorning, the twins expected a lull before the lunch crowd came in. In

154

fact it was so quiet behind the counter that Elizabeth decided to go back and talk to Mr. Campbell in the stockroom, leaving Jessica to man the counter with Mindy.

Jessica was making herself an ice-cream float when the door opened and Annie Sue sauntered in. Jessica thought the girl had never looked so smug—or so unfriendly. Her dark hair was hanging loose around her shoulders, and she was wearing a kelly green sweater and a blue denim skirt. Jessica thought the girl could be pretty if she only smiled.

"Hi," Jessica said warily, setting aside the glass she had just filled with ice cream.

Annie Sue strolled casually up to the counter, made a great production out of climbing onto a stool and setting her handbag down, and continued to stare at Jessica the whole time.

"Can I help you?" Jessica asked after an uncomfortable silence.

Annie Sue looked at her for another minute before answering. "Have fun last night, Jessica?" she asked, taking a little plastic compact out of her bag. She opened it and began eyeing herself in the miniature mirror.

"Yes," Jessica said, trying to keep her temper. "As a matter of fact, I did, Annie Sue. Why do you ask?"

Annie Sue raised her eyebrows and snapped the compact shut. "Oh—just curious, I guess," she said smoothly. She studied Jessica, her eyes flicking from Jessica's hairstyle to the baggy sweater and narrow skirt she was wearing beneath her apron. "That's a nice headband," Annie Sue said.

Jessica's hands flew up to her head. "Thanks," she said. She couldn't figure this girl out. What was Annie Sue up to? Why had she come into Walker's in the first place? For some reason the way she kept staring made Jessica feel uneasy. She wished Annie Sue would cut it out.

"I was just kind of wondering," Annie Sue said, fiddling with a straw, "if your aunt and uncle knew you were out so late last night, Jessica. Somehow I didn't think the Walkers were big on the idea of their wonderful nieces running around town unchaperoned after eleven at night."

"My aunt and uncle didn't know I was out," Jessica said in a low, terse voice.

"Ooooooohhhh," Annie Sue said, pretending to look surprised. "Really? You mean to say you've been keeping it a little secret—just between you and that carnie you were hanging out with?"

Jessica felt her face burn. "Alex isn't a carnie," she snapped. "His father owns the carnival. He's only working there during his spring vacation from college."

Again Annie Sue's eyebrows shot up. "Oh, I see," she said in a high, thin voice. "Well, that *does* make a difference, doesn't it? I'm sure that would make your aunt and uncle feel a whole lot better about things, don't you think?"

"My aunt and uncle aren't going to find out about it," Jessica said, struggling to keep the fury out of her voice. "Look, Annie Sue, ever since we got here you've been treating my sister and me like we've got the plague or something. I have no idea why you hate us so much, but—"

"Hate you?" Annie Sue interrupted with a horrible, artificial little laugh. "No one *hates* anyone here, Jessica." She glanced meaningfully toward the back of the store. "I suppose if I happened to say something to the Walkers about seeing you last night it would really only be for their own good. I mean, your uncle *is* the mayor,

Jessica. I wouldn't want his reputation ruined just because of you."

"Then don't ruin it," Jessica snapped. She had taken just about as much as she could from this girl, and her patience was running out.

"I really like that headband," Annie Sue repeated, staring at Jessica's hair. "Have you got another one like it?"

Jessica stared at her. "No," she said, wondering if the girl was off her rocker. "It was handmade in L.A. A friend gave it to me," she said.

"Really?" Annie Sue looked at the headband with increasing interest. "Can I have it?" she asked casually.

Jessica stared at her. "*Have* it?" she repeated incredulously. "But—it was a present," she said. Lila had given her the headband, and it was one of her favorites. The last thing on earth she wanted to do was to give it to Annie Sue Sawyer!

"So what?" Annie Sue said, shifting on the stool. "Give it to me."

Jessica stared at her, a terrible sensation in her stomach. "And I suppose if I don't, you'll just happen to mention to my aunt and uncle that you saw me out last night, right?"

Annie Sue smiled. It was a cold, terrible smile that made Jessica incredibly angry. "That's right," she said, hopping off the stool. Elizabeth was coming toward them, a baffled expression on her face. "Hurry up," Annie Sue muttered. "Give me your headband, Jessica."

Jessica didn't stop to think. She yanked her headband off, crumpled it up, and dropped it into the girl's outstretched hand.

"Thanks," Annie Sue said, the smile fading from her face. "I'll be back." With that she turned on her heel and walked out of the store.

"The lights in here must be doing weird things to my eyes," Elizabeth said, coming behind the counter and staring at her sister. "Did I just see you give your headband to Miss Inhospitality, or am I cracking up?"

Jessica felt her eyes fill with tears. "You saw what you thought you saw," she said shortly. "I don't want to talk about it, Liz."

Elizabeth was quiet for a minute. "I think," she said finally, "I smell trouble. Are you OK, Jess?"

Jessica sighed. "Liz, I think I'm being black-mailed."

"Blackmailed? For what?"

Jessica was close to tears. "Annie Sue saw me

out with Alex last night. I didn't want to tell you because I knew you'd be furious. But I couldn't help it! We were just over by the bike rack. I was unlocking my bike and was just about to head home, and there she was!" Jessica covered her face with her hands. "It was horrible. And now she's threatening to tell Aunt Shirley and Uncle Herman."

Elizabeth looked horrified. "What a brat!" she exclaimed. She put her arms around her twin. "Don't worry, Jess. I'm not mad at you. I mean, I *was* mad at you for sneaking out, but you couldn't help getting spied on. And you can't help the fact that Annie Sue seems to get her kicks by torturing us."

Tears spilled down Jessica's cheeks. "You're so nice," she choked out miserably. "I thought you'd be ready to strangle me."

Elizabeth shook her head. "We're going to have to stick together, Jess. There's no point in the two of us fighting. We've got enough to worry about as it is."

"Well," Jessica said, taking a deep, quavering breath, "as long as we've got stuff she wants, maybe she'll keep quiet."

"I hate the thought of actually giving that girl

things, though." Elizabeth sighed. "But I don't see any alternative. Anyone else I'd figure we could reason with. But from the way she's behaved all week, my guess is that she's exactly the sort of creep who really *would* tell Aunt Shirley and Uncle Herman. And then what would we do?"

The twins stared at each other. It was too awful a thought to consider. They just had to hope they could manage somehow to keep Annie Sue quiet.

The dreadful thing was that they realized they were dependent on Annie Sue's every whim. No matter what she asked them to do for the rest of their visit, they would be forced to go along with it. And even giving in to her was no guarantee that she would keep quiet about what she had seen!

On Friday evening the twins went out to dinner with their aunt and uncle at a small restaurant called Holinshed's, about twenty minutes from Walkersville. Holinshed's was actually an old inn with a big, homey dining room serving wonderful fried chicken, dumplings, mashed potatoes, and, according to Mrs. Walker, the best chocolate cake anywhere in Kansas.

"I can't believe you girls are really going back to California Monday morning," Mrs. Walker said, looking up from her menu, her eyes misty. "I can't tell you how wonderful it's been having you visit."

"It's been wonderful for us, too," Elizabeth said.

Jessica ran her eyes down the menu. The truth was she had lost her appetite. All she could think about were the things she had been forced to silently hand over to that terrible Annie Sue since Thursday morning. Her headband. A plastic sport watch. A rhinestone pin. And Annie Sue had extracted promises for several things that Jessica just didn't happen to have with her, including—and this hurt most of all—her red cowboy boots. Jessica was too angry to feel like eating, and she had to force herself to order dinner with the rest. At this point they'd probably drag her off to Dr. Bloomfield at the least sign of loss of appetite, since they already thought something was wrong with her.

"You know, we haven't even asked you girls about the square dance on Sunday night," Mrs.

Walker said suddenly. "It's really a wonderful event. I think you'd both get quite a kick out of it. Don't you think so, Herman? It's held in the town hall," she added, turning back to the twins. "They really do it up well, and just about everyone in the whole town comes. We thought it would be nice if the four of us went together."

The twins exchanged glances.

"Is something wrong?" their uncle asked, concerned.

"Uh—it's just—" Jessica began, staring helplessly at her sister.

"We've been planning on going to the square dance," Elizabeth filled in for her. "But we both accepted invitations already. We were planning to double-date."

"Double-date?" Mrs. Walker repeated blankly. "Girls, why didn't you say something about this to us? Who are these boys?"

"Shirley," her husband said, putting his hand warningly over hers on the table. He lowered his voice, looking at the twins with a frown. "Girls, I must say this surprises me," he said slowly. "I'm sure both your aunt and I would have preferred it if you had discussed your plans with us before solidifying them."

Elizabeth swallowed. "We—I guess we're at fault," she murmured. "You see, at home we're used to being able to go out with anyone we please. So you see, I think we just sort of assumed—"

"Can you at least tell us who you've agreed to go with?" Mrs. Walker asked in a low voice.

The twins filled them in on the details, explaining that Alex and Brad were twins. They were sons of the owner of the carnival, and nice, smart, respectable boys whom they would be safe with.

"We haven't even met them," Mrs. Walker said, distraught. "Anyway, Jessica, when have you found time to get to know Alex? I had no idea you'd been spending time with boys since you arrived!"

"I don't really think this is the best time or place to discuss this," Mr. Walker said quietly. "Girls, this is something I think your aunt and I will have to discuss alone before we can come to any kind of decision."

Jessica's eyes widened. "You mean we may not be able to go?" she asked.

"Let's just wait and see," Mrs. Walker said, looking upset. "Your uncle is right, though. We need to talk this over very carefully before making any final decision." She picked her fork up meaningfully. "Now, why don't we just enjoy our dinner and not worry about this right now?"

Jessica looked with complete disinterest at the food the waiter had just set down before her. She hadn't been hungry before, and now she felt sick to her stomach. She couldn't believe her aunt and uncle could really do this to them. It would be just too cruel.

Twelve

On their last date Elizabeth and Brad had made plans to meet on Saturday afternoon at two-thirty in front of town hall, but when she arrived he was nowhere to be seen. She slipped her sunglasses on and sat down on the bench in front of the building to wait for him.

"Liz!" a high, feminine voice called.

She looked up to see Annie Sue approaching, a smirk on her pretty face. "Oh, hello," Elizabeth said in a flat voice.

"You don't sound very happy to see me," Annie Sue said with a little pout. She stood, staring down at Elizabeth, scrutinizing her in a way that gave Elizabeth the creeps.

"I don't like what you're doing to Jessica," Elizabeth said, deciding not to waste words. "I think it's unfair. As a matter of fact, I think you've been cruel to both of us since we got here, and I really don't understand why, Annie Sue. We wanted to be friends. We wanted a chance to get to know you and the other girls in Walkersville. Only you wouldn't give us the opportunity."

Annie Sue looked away and took a deep breath. For a minute Elizabeth thought she had broken through to the girl, that Annie Sue was actually going to apologize. But the next instant Annie Sue's face had hardened again.

"I like the sunglasses you're wearing," she said in a threatening voice. "You wouldn't mind lending them to me for the day, would you?"

"As a matter of fact, I would mind," Elizabeth retorted. "I need them, Annie Sue."

The girl raised her eyebrows coolly. "More than you need me to keep quiet about your sister?" she asked.

Elizabeth stared at her. "I really don't understand you, Annie Sue," she murmured, taking her glasses off and handing them to her. "How come you hate us so much?"

Annie Sue dropped the glasses into her handbag. Without answering she turned and stormed off, leaving Elizabeth staring after her. She was so upset about Annie Sue that she barely noticed Brad coming up to join her.

"Hey," he said, leaning forward to tousle her hair. "You look about nine thousand miles away. Am I late?"

Elizabeth shook her head. "No, I was a few minutes early." She tried to smile, uncertain whether or not to burden Brad by telling him what Annie Sue had been doing to her and Jessica.

"You look like you need to be cheered up," Brad said. "Which means you may not be all that crazy about coming with me to the corral to do my brother a favor and get things set for tonight. He's off showing Midnight to a buyer again," he added.

Elizabeth smiled. "I don't need cheering up. And I'd be happy to come with you to the corral," she assured him. She couldn't help noticing how nice Brad looked. He was wearing straight-legged blue jeans with a rawhide belt and a plaid flannel shirt. He looked very rugged, more like Alex than usual, she thought with a smile. She was also relieved to note that while she registered how handsome he was, her stomach didn't do the little dive it had before when she looked at him. She still thought he was cute, but that dizzy, unsettling attraction she had felt for him seemed to be gone.

Still, she did enjoy Brad's company. They talked as they strolled over to the carnival. Elizabeth explained what had happened with Annie Sue. Brad looked concerned—and angry. "That girl deserves to have someone give her a good talking to," he muttered to himself. "Jessica must be furious," he added.

Elizabeth nodded. "She is." Then she giggled. "It's just lucky she came equipped. Only my sister would have enough accessories to keep a whole town satisfied!"

Brad didn't say anything more. They had reached the corral, and he stopped to examine a protruding nail on the gate. "Liz, I have to pick up here. Would you do me a favor and run into the stable? There's a hammer hanging up on the corkboard," he said, touching the nail with his hand.

Elizabeth complied. She was gone only for a minute, but when she came back with the hammer she stopped short, her heart beating faster. Brad was doubled up in front of the gate, swearing and holding his right hand cupped in his left. An expression of severe pain contorted his handsome features.

"Are you all right?" she asked, hurrying toward him.

"I don't know how I managed to do that," Brad said, wincing as he showed her his right hand. "Damn," he muttered, staring down at the gash in his palm. "Liz, see if there's a first-aid box in the stables, will you?"

Fortunately the first-aid kit was sitting on a small table in the makeshift stables, and it appeared to be complete. "Do you think you need stitches?" she asked, looking closely at the cut.

"I don't think so. The bleeding seems to have slowed down a little," Brad said, wincing when she poured antiseptic on the cut. "Thanks," he said gratefully when she had helped him bandage his hand. "I can't believe I did that! I turned to move away and left my hand on the gate. It swung closed and the nail ripped my hand."

"As long as you think it's OK," Elizabeth said. "Have you had a tetnus shot recently?"

"Just a couple of months ago, so I'm all right." He stretched his left hand out to touch her cheek. "You're such a sweet girl," he said softly. "So serious sometimes! Don't worry about my hand. It's going to be fine."

Elizabeth got to her feet. "I think I'd better get going soon," she said regretfully. "My aunt and uncle are planning dinner early tonight, and I promised I'd be home to help."

Brad got to his feet, too, looking down at his bandaged hand. "I hope Alex gets back soon," he said. "I'm not going to be much use around here till this thing stops throbbing."

Elizabeth glanced down at her watch. "Oh, speaking of Alex," she said thoughtfully. "We may have a problem about tomorrow night. My aunt and uncle are really being strict about things. I think they feel uncomfortable about us going out with people they haven't met."

"Oh, well," Brad said, looking strangely relieved. "Maybe we can all get together some other time."

"Wait a minute!" Elizabeth said. "We don't have to cancel our plans yet. You still want to go, don't you?"

"Uh—sure," Brad said, avoiding her gaze.

"We thought it might be best just to have you guys come over to the house first—you know, placate my aunt and uncle, show them you're not criminals." Elizabeth smiled. "That is, if they give us the OK tonight at dinner. We'll have to let you know tomorrow, I guess. Will I be able to find you here?"

"Sure," Brad said, fiddling with the bandage on his hand. Elizabeth thought he gave her a peculiar look, but she decided she had just imagined it. Maybe his hand was hurting him. Or maybe he was more sensitive than she had realized and resented her aunt and uncle's worry.

But Elizabeth did know one thing for sure then. There was no romantic spark between her and Brad Parker. They were friends, and nothing more.

Perhaps if she could assure her aunt and uncle of that, they would be less likely to object to their plans for the square dance the following night.

"Listen, girls," Mr. Walker said seriously, pacing back and forth in the living room. Jessica and Elizabeth were sitting on the couch, and their aunt was standing near the mantel, looking at them all with utmost anxiety. "We've been talking about nothing else since last night," Uncle Herman told them. "We're very, very reluctant to make ultimatums. After all, you two are guests here, and we want you to enjoy yourselves. And we realize that when you're at home you have certain kinds of freedom that have been denied to you here. But we still feel that in good conscience we simply cannot let you go to the dance tomorrow night with boys whose family we don't know or even know anything about. It would be one thing if we could come along with you, if you merely invited the boys to join us. But to let you go alone—well, we feel it just wouldn't be right."

Jessica's face went through a series of expressions—first disbelief, then anger, then frustration. "Aunt Shirley," she burst out imploringly, turning to her, "can't you see how we feel? We *know* these boys. We know they're really nice, that they wouldn't do anything out of line. Please—" she begged.

Mrs. Walker said unhappily, "Jess, darling, we just can't allow it. I mean, put yourself in our places, dear. Here we are, having promised your parents we'd look out for you, take complete care of you while you're here. And in your condition, I'm not even sure you should be going to the dance at all, let alone with some stranger!"

"What condition?" Jessica asked.

"You know, dear. Your sleeping problem."

"I don't *have* a sleeping problem!" Jessica wailed. "Listen, I'm *begging* you two. *Please* let us go," she said urgently.

But Mr. and Mrs. Walker were shaking their heads. Elizabeth put her hand on her sister's arm, but the combination of things she had borne recently proved too great for Jessica, whose eyes flooded with tears. The next minute she stormed out of the living room into the bedroom, slamming the door behind her so hard the house shook.

"Let me just go try to calm her down," Elizabeth said, giving her aunt and uncle an apologetic look as she hastened after Jessica.

"I can't stand it. I just can't stand it," Jessica was muttering as Elizabeth opened the door to the bedroom. Jessica was in front of her dresser, yanking drawers open and tearing through the contents of her drawers as if she were searching for something vital. At last she pulled out a pair of jeans and proceeded to change into them with lightning speed.

"Something tells me that you're planning another exodus," Elizabeth said dryly. "You've got that I'm-going-to-sneak-out-of-the-house-and-give-my-twin-sister-a-heart-attack look on your face."

"I can't help it," Jessica fumed. "I promised Alex I'd meet him at the corral at eighty-thirty. I'll just have to go early and let him know I'll never see him again." Tears came flooding back at the injustice of the situation. "I was so excited about tomorrow night, too. It just doesn't seem fair!"

"It does seem like they could be a little more understanding," Elizabeth admitted. "But I guess we're really kind of stuck. Anyway, it's just for another day. We're going back home on Monday," Elizabeth reminded her.

"But that's the whole point!" Jessica wailed. "After that I won't be able to see Alex anymore. It'll be too late! Liz, I don't think I can stand it. I finally meet someone I really care about, and I'm not even allowed to go to a stupid square dance with him!"

Elizabeth didn't know what to say. She knew her sister was right. It was a terrible situation. She felt for her. It wasn't so bad for her and Brad. There wasn't that strong a feeling there. But Jessica and Alex obviously cared for each other. "Just try not to do anything crazy," she said sympathetically, watching Jessica fasten her silver necklace around her neck.

"I won't," Jessica said dully. "As far as I can

tell, there's nothing I can do anymore, except explain what's happened to Alex and say good-bye to him." She sniffed as she grabbed her jacket. "Don't worry," she added dully. "I won't be late."

Elizabeth didn't know what to say. She could tell how upset her sister was, but she couldn't think of anything to do to make things better for her.

All she could do was watch Jessica slip out, and hope against hope that her aunt and uncle didn't discover she had sneaked out to the carnival without their permission.

Thirteen

Jessica bit her lip as she approached the corral. She was fighting hard for control, knowing how hard the next moments were going to be. She still couldn't believe it was happening—that she had to tell Alex their plans for the dance the next night were off and that they'd never see each other again.

"Alex," she called as she approached the corral. Her voice caught a little at the sight of him. He looked even more handsome than usual in a white flannel shirt and black denim jeans. His eyes lit up when he saw her.

"Jess!" he cried, hurrying over and giving her a quick, affectionate kiss on the forehead. "I'm so glad to see you!"

"Alex," Jessica began again, hating to put off the inevitable longer than she had to.

But Alex cut her off. "Listen, I've got wonderful news," he said happily. "There's a man in town named Sawyer who wants to buy Midnight. He seems really nice, and the best thing is that he'll be showing Midnight in Kansas City once in a while, so I'll be able to see him."

Jessica stared at him. "Sawyer?" she repeated. "Alex—"

"But here's the thing," he cut in again, obviously too excited to wait to finish his story. "He wants me to meet him in a few minutes, someplace we can sit down. He's going to introduce me to his business partner or something—" Alex broke off after looking at his watch. "Listen, I've got to go meet him. My dad promised he'd send someone over to replace me, but the guy hasn't shown up. I don't want to risk having the deal fall through. Can you keep an eye on the corral for just about ten minutes? Just make sure the kids walk or trot and that they stay off Midnight."

Jessica opened her mouth to answer, but Alex was already off. *Darn*, she thought unhappily, strolling over to the corral gate, climbing up, and perching on a post. She didn't want to be away from Five Elms long. She had promised Elizabeth she'd be back soon. Well, she assured herself, he had said it would just be five or ten minutes. She supposed that it couldn't make too much difference.

Mr. Sawyer was buying Midnight! Jessica wrinkled her nose at the prospect. It seemed unfair for that beautiful stallion to belong to Annie Sue Sawyer. Jessica shuddered when she recalled the girl's annoying boasts about what a great rider she was. Just thinking about Annie Sue made her cringe.

To her horror, she saw Annie Sue strolling toward the corral, deep in thought. Jessica tried to turn so her face wasn't visible, but it was too late. The girl had seen her and was walking toward her.

"Great," Jessica said out loud, wincing. All she really needed to cap off a truly dismal day was another encounter with Annie Sue.

"Hi, Jessica," Annie Sue said in a wheedling voice as she walked right up to the corral, looking at Jessica with smug satisfaction. "I suppose you've heard the news," she added, twirling a lock of dark hair around her finger.

"What news?" Jessica asked flatly.

"Why, about Midnight," Annie Sue said.

"Daddy's buying him for me—for my birthday. So I'll be able to ride him whenever I want," she added. She leaned over the corral gate and patted the black stallion's neck. Midnight shied away, his ears flicking the way they did when he was nervous.

Jessica fought to control herself. "That's nice," she said unemotionally. If only she could tell the girl what she really thought of her! But she had promised her parents she would behave herself—that she would remember how much her aunt and uncle cared what the people in town thought of them. Swallowing hard, she turned away from Annie Sue and looked sadly at Midnight. *Poor thing,* she thought. *What a life you're going to have from now on!*

"I like that necklace you're wearing, Jessica," Annie Sue remarked when it became apparent that she hadn't been able to get a rise out of Jessica by talking about the stallion. "Don't you think it would look nice with what I'm wearing?"

Jessica eyed Annie Sue's flowered blouse, tan chinos, and suede jacket with contempt. "No," she said finally. "I think it would look"—she pretended to search for the right word—"kind of *foul,*" she said finally. She loved the big silver beads she was wearing and had no intention of giving Annie Sue the necklace.

Annie Sue's eyes burned with anger. "Give it to me," she said harshly, reaching out. "You know what I'll do if you don't!"

Jessica was so angry she felt tears well up in her eyes. But she knew it would be giving in to let Annie Sue see how she felt. "Here," she said, unclasping the necklace and dropping it into the girl's outstretched hand. "But you know, Annie Sue, we're only going to be in town until Monday morning. What are you going to do for kicks when we're gone?"

Annie Sue glared at her. "I'm going to teach Midnight how to jump," she declared. "In fact, I think I may just as well get started right now." She opened the corral gate and stormed over to the stallion, who backed up nervously, neighing loudly.

"Annie Sue, you can't ride him now," Jessica said as patiently as she could. "For one thing, Alex—"

"Oh, who cares about Alex?" Annie Sue cried. "I can ride him if I want to. He practically belongs to me. I can do whatever I feel like!" The next minute she was grabbing the stallion's mane, trying to clamber up onto the horse's unsaddled back.

Jessica was getting alarmed. "Annie Sue, don't!" she exclaimed, jumping off the post and hurrying over to grab Midnight's bridle. "He's not even saddled! And he's not entirely trained yet," she reminded her. "He's really temperamental. It's dangerous for you to ride him. Please," she added, practically begging.

Annie Sue flipped her hair back imperiously, and with a little jump pulled herself up onto the horse. "Don't tell me what to do, Miss High and Mighty," she snapped. "I've been riding horses since I was three. I know exactly how to handle him! *Now get out of my way.*"

Jessica was still clinging to Midnight's bridle, trying to calm the frightened animal by stroking his nose. But her efforts were defeated by Annie Sue, who leaned forward and yanked on the reins in exactly the way Alex had warned Jessica not to. The stallion reared back, dancing nervously to the left.

"Whoa," Annie Sue said ineffectually, pulling back even harder on the reins. "Stop it, horse. Stop jerking around like that."

"Annie Sue, you've got to get off him!" Jessica cried. She was losing her hold on the bridle. Much as Jessica disliked Annie Sue, she didn't want to see her in real danger. And Jessica knew very well how dangerous Midnight could be if he became frightened.

Annie Sue was beginning to turn pale. "He's acting really weird!" she exclaimed as Midnight kept pulling his neck back and tossing it wildly, trying to free himself from the pressure on his mouth.

Jessica's heart began to pound as her hand was torn loose from the bridle. Annie Sue was in danger, and Jessica had to figure out a way to get her off the horse and back on the ground. But how? *If only Alex were here*, she thought desperately. *He'd know what to do*. Annie Sue was beginning to cry a little. Her terror was infectious, and Jessica again wished desperately that Alex were there to help.

But Alex wasn't there. And just as Jessica was making an attempt to grab the bridle, she heard a terrible crash from somewhere behind the stables as if a large piece of metal had fallen to the pavement. That was all Midnight needed. Nervous and agitated to begin with, the sudden noise was too much for his nerves, and the next thing Jessica knew he was galloping around the corral, the terrified Annie Sue barely hanging on and screaming bloody murder! Jessica knew that at any minute he could bolt and jump over the fences endangering not only Annie Sue but many other people.

Jessica's anger at Annie Sue dissolved in the wake of the new emotion she was feeling then—fear. Fear and pity for the screaming girl whose face reflected the terror she was feeling. Jessica knew she had to do something to save her, and she didn't have a second to lose!

Elizabeth was pacing back and forth uneasily in the bedroom, wondering what could be keeping her sister. She kept staring at her watch, sighing, pacing around some more, and asking herself, for the millionth time, what was going to happen when her aunt and uncle found out Jessica had sneaked out of the house.

She didn't have much longer to wonder.

"Girls?" her aunt's familiar voice inquired. The next minute the bedroom door opened. "We're so sorry we had to have an argument about tomorrow night," Mrs. Walker said unhappily. "We'd really like to talk it over with you again. Your uncle and I think we may have been too—" She broke off in midsentence. "Why, where's Jessica?" she asked with surprise.

"Uh—she's—uh—" Elizabeth felt her face turn red. The bathroom door was wide open this time, and Jessica was nowhere to be seen. "She left," she concluded weakly, sitting down on the bed.

"Left? Left where? Herman!" Mrs. Walker called, clutching her heart. "Something terrible has happened—Jessica's run away!"

"She hasn't run away," Elizabeth cried. "She's just sort of—uh, she's just gone to the carnival to explain to Alex that we can't go out with him and his brother tomorrow night."

"You mean to tell me she just *went*? Without even asking us?" Mrs. Walker shrieked.

"Well, she thought you'd say no. And we didn't want those poor guys to just be waiting for us tomorrow night," Elizabeth pointed out.

"What's happened? Who's run away?" Mr. Walker exclaimed, rushing into the bedroom.

"Jessica," his wife said. "She sneaked off to the carnival without our permission!"

"To the carnival?" Mr. Walker repeated. "But—"

"I think we should jump in the car right now and go get her," Mrs. Walker declared. "There's no telling what could happen to that girl, wandering around by herself on a Saturday night. It's just out of the question. Herman. Let's go."

Elizabeth sighed. She wished she could convince her aunt and uncle that Jessica wasn't in any danger. But Elizabeth knew that wouldn't satisfy them. Grabbing her jacket, she hurried after them to the garage.

Something told her there was going to be a scene when they arrived at the carnival. And the very least she could do would be to lend her twin moral support!

Jessica took a deep breath. "Please let this work," she thought, trying to quell the terror she was feeling. Grabbing the pommel on the saddle of the dapple horse nearest her, she pulled herself up and grabbed the reins. Midnight was running in wild, increasingly wide circles around the corral, pawing the ground and throwing his head back wildly. Jessica had to get to Annie Sue before the stallion threw her. Everything was happening so quickly Jessica barely had time to think. She was vaguely aware that a crowd was gathering outside the corral, and she knew that Alex or his father

188

would probably be there at any moment, but in the meantime there wasn't a second to lose.

Jessica knew she had to quiet Midnight down fast. The only way she could think to do that was to get to him, and use the technique Alex had showed her to calm him.

But, how was she going to catch hold of him? And even if she could, would she calm him before it was too late?

Fourteen

Alex had to push his way through the crowd gathered around the corral in order to find out what was going on. When he saw Jessica galloping after Midnight, his heart leaped in his throat. "Good Lord," he cried. The next instant he was jumping over the fence into the corral and charging after Jessica and Annie Sue.

Jessica was riding with more intense concentration than she ever had before. Almost intuitively she grasped that she had to get Midnight against the corral fence. Riding in front of him, she cut him off, slowing him down long enough so that she could lean over and grab the reins. "Hang on, Annie Sue," she said. "Just drop the reins. Let me take over."

Annie Sue stared at her, her face drained of

color. "Help me, Jess," she shouted. "He's going to throw me. I'll be killed!"

"No, you won't," Jessica said grimly. "Just sit tight." She took a deep breath, still clinging to both sets of reins and pulling her own horse alongside Midnight. "I'm going to try to calm him down," she called to the terrified girl. "Sit as still as you can."

Annie Sue gasped. "How are you going to do it?"

"Just watch," Jessica said. She released her own set of reins and reached over to pat Midnight's neck. The stallion shimmied over a step or two, but she kept patting him. "Sit still, Annie Sue," she urged. The frightened girl obeyed.

By now Alex had run up alongside and grabbed Midnight's bridle. "Jess, I've got him. Everything's under control," Alex called. "Annie Sue, I'm getting on behind you," he added. The next minute he had mounted the skittish horse, leaning around Annie Sue and patting his neck. "Whoa, boy," he said. "Take it easy. Whoa!"

Jessica breathed a long sigh of relief as she backed her own horse up and followed Alex and Annie Sue. Now that Alex was there, she knew everything was OK.

They rode slowly around the corral to cool the horse down. A huge crowd was cheering them on; Annie Sue's father right at the front. Jessica finally slipped off her horse and then reached up to help Annie Sue. "Come on," she said. "I'll help you down, Annie Sue."

The girl was so frightened she just hung on to the saddle, staring down at Jessica, as Alex dismounted behind her. "Come on," Jessica said again. And this time Annie Sue slid off the horse. The girl's face was stained with tears. The crowd burst into a roar of applause.

"You saved my life," Annie Sue said. The next minute she threw her arms around Jessica's neck and gave her an enormous hug.

"What's going on here?" Mr. Walker exclaimed, rushing up to the crowd with a look of confusion and panic on his face. "Has someone been hurt?" Mrs. Walker and Elizabeth were right behind him.

"Your niece and Alex over there just rescued my daughter," Mr. Sawyer boomed, one arm around Jessica and the other around Annie Sue.

"Rescued her?" Mrs. Walker looked faint. "What happened?" she asked.

"It was all my fault," Alex said, approaching them. He looked miserable. "I should never have left the corral for a second. I just wanted to say a word or two to Mr. Sawyer—"

"It was my fault, son," Mr. Sawyer interrupted him. "I should never have taken you away from your work. You made it clear that you had responsibilities, and I insisted."

"*I* was the one who was supposed to keep an eye on the corral, though," Jessica moaned. "I should never have allowed you to get on Midnight!" she added, turning to Annie Sue.

Annie Sue wiped the tears from her face. "What a dope I am." She sighed. "What an incredible dope! Jessica tried to keep me off Midnight," she explained to the crowd. "She really did. But I just wouldn't listen. I thought I knew enough about horses to handle him, but I obviously don't. He just started going wild when he heard that crash."

"Yeah," Jessica said suddenly, mystified. "What made that terrible noise?"

"It was one of the poles that holds up the awning over the office adjoining the stable," Alex told her. "It got loose somehow, and it came crashing down, right onto the pavement. Metal hitting rock, just the sort of noise that makes a skittish horse really crazy."

"Well, I think both these young people deserve a big round of applause," Mr. Sawyer said, pushing Jessica and Alex forward a little. "You don't often see this kind of courage and selfless initiative. You two really ought to be proud of yourselves."

Jessica blushed and stared at the ground. The whole thing had happened so quickly she'd had no idea what she was doing. She had just known, almost instinctively, that she had to calm Midnight down. She had to save her.

Annie Sue looked shyly at her, her brown eyes shiny. "I think if anyone here knew the truth they'd realize that what you did was much more than brave," she murmured. "You put yourself in danger trying to get me off that horse, Jessica. After the way I've treated you . . ."

"It's OK," Jessica said, embarrassed.

Annie Sue fumbled with the clasp on the silver necklace she had taken from Jessica less than an hour earlier. "Here," she whispered, handing it back. "This is yours."

Jessica cleared her throat. "It's OK," she repeated. "That's what friends are for, Annie Sue. You're welcome to borrow my necklace, and all the other stuff! It's really OK."

"I don't know which I ought to do first," she murmured. "Thank you, or apologize to you."

Jessica laughed. "First," she said, turning back to the crowd, "I think we better do something about my aunt and uncle. They look like they've got a couple questions to ask me, and considering the way things have been going around here, I really can't blame them!"

Mrs. Walker threw her arms around Jessica. "We should probably scold you for sneaking out of the house, but, Jessica, we're so proud of you for being such a heroine tonight that nothing else seems to matter!" she exclaimed.

"I think," Mr. Walker said, patting Jessica on the shoulder, "it's high time the four of us sat down and had a good long talk. But before we do a thing, let me just tell you that I'm really proud of you, Jessica. You and your friend Alex really used your heads, and your courage, this evening!"

"Thanks, Uncle Herman," Jessica said. She couldn't help brightening when she heard Alex's name included in her uncle's praise. Maybe that meant there was still a chance to salvage their date for the square dance!

Annie Sue managed to get Jessica to herself while Alex and Mr. Sawyer were talking earnestly to the Walkers about what had happened with Midnight. They were both still a little dazed from their frenetic ride. Jessica plopped down on the ground behind the stables and wiped her brow with her hand. Annie Sue came over to join her.

"Good," the girl said, her brown eyes serious. "I finally get a chance to apologize!"

Jessica looked up at her. "You don't have to apologize, Annie Sue," she said slowly. "But I am curious about one thing. Can you explain why you and your friends were so upset about Elizabeth and me? Did you get some kind of weird impression about us before we came?"

Annie Sue dropped down beside Jessica and looked thoughtfully down at her hands. "Well, it's kind of strange," she said softly. "The thing is, Jessica, ever since I can remember I've always been . . . well, this is going to sound dumb, but I've always been sort of the leader in Walkersville with the kids my age. You know what I mean?"

"I think so," Jessica said.

"Well, I've always had a lot of influence with my girlfriends. I guess I've grown up kind of spoiled. I'm an only child, and my parents have given me everything I ever wanted. Like Midnight." She sighed. "All I had to do was tell Daddy how beautiful I thought he was, and he made sure he got him for me." She looked at Jessica. "The thing is, I've always been incredibly insecure, too. I've always felt like the girls in town just like me because . . . I don't know why. I was afraid of you and Liz." She took a deep breath. "The way your aunt and uncle talked about you—you know, making you sound so clever, so glamorous—I was convinced all the kids in town would think you two were the greatest, and I was jealous. And when I saw you talking to Dennis—"

"I wasn't really flirting with him," Jessica interrupted. "I mean, I guess it kind of looked that way, but I was just—well, that's just the way I am with guys, I guess."

"See, the way I saw it, you *were* flirting. But I guess I had expected, or feared, that. I assumed you and Elizabeth would both be really experienced with guys. Like Alex," she added, shaking her head with a smile. "Alex is the kind of guy I always assumed would never pay much attention to me. I've never gone out with an older guy or anyone from out of town. So I guess I was a little jealous of you. I think I was even more jealous watching you with Alex than with Dennis. I know Dennis loves me," she added softly. "And I love him, too. But we've known each other since we were about six. We'll probably end up getting married. It just isn't always that exciting, you know?"

"Wow," Jessica said. "You guys have known each other since you were six?" Suddenly she felt a little sorry for Annie Sue. She sounded trapped, and more than a little confused.

"I love Walkersville," Annie Sue added, looking around her and hugging her knees up to her chest. "I love the thought of settling here. I don't want you to get me wrong, Jessica. Most of the time I'm really happy. For some reason you and Elizabeth just brought out the insecurity in me. You made me doubt everything. Not that you *did* anything. You just had to show up here, looking the way you do. Oh, come on," she said quickly, seeing the protesting expression on Jessica's face. "Just think how glamorous and exciting the way you look is compared to most of us!" She blushed. "Maybe that's why I wanted all your things, your necklaces and headbands and all that."

"You know you're welcome to borrow any of that stuff," Jessica told her. She couldn't believe her own ears. It wasn't like her to offer her favorite possessions to a stranger. But she found herself sympathizing with this girl. The experience they had been through that evening had made her feel close to Annie Sue. She thought she could understand the insecurity the girl was describing, and she wanted to show she was willing to forgive her and to make amends.

Annie Sue blushed. "I plan to give it all back, of course," she said. "Jessica, I've learned my lesson. The truth is that I've got to be able to be happy with myself the way I am. And basically I am. I owe you both an enormous apology." She shuddered. "When I think back now on the way I treated you . . ."

"You *were* unfriendly," Jessica said truthfully. She giggled. "That day at the farm . . ."

Annie Sue covered her face with her hands. "I can't believe I did that! Jessica, it makes me want to die now. I made Janie torture you guys all morning and then convinced my friends to join me in humiliating you by not showing up at lunch." She shuddered again. "My grandmother almost killed me. I think even she saw through the weak excuse I gave her."

"Well, we don't have much time left in Walkersville," Jessica said slowly, "but I know I'd still like the chance to get to know you and your friends. And I'm sure Elizabeth would like the opportunity, too."

"You know what?" Annie Sue exclaimed, snapping her fingers. "I'm going to ask my dad if we can invite you back to the house tonight; we'll have a party. I'll get Dennis to round up a bunch of guys, and Mary and Susie can get all the girls. And we'll have a chance to get to know each other before the square dance tomorrow night."

"It would be fun coming over to your house," Jessica said enthusiastically. "If my aunt and uncle don't mind."

"Oh, we'll bring them, too!" Annie Sue said. She blushed again. "If you come over, I'll give back all that stuff I made you give me. And maybe"—she looked really shy—"I can make it up to you by giving you some stuff from Walkersville. I'm not really sure what I've got that you'd want, but we can look around."

Jessica laughed. "We can trade," she suggested. "You can give me something that's a hundred percent Walkersville, and I'll give you something a hundred percent Sweet Valley."

Annie Sue looked delighted. But the next minute her expression grew sober. "I still shiver every time I think about what happened tonight on Midnight," she admitted. "You know, I'm going to need a lot of help learning how to ride Midnight—and how to take care of him. I want him to have a good home here. And I want you to come visit him, and me, whenever you can."

Jessica gave the girl an impulsive hug. "I'll show you what Alex showed me," she said happily. "And the next time you ride him should be a lot more fun than this time was!"

"I sure hope so," Annie Sue said, scrambling to her feet. She put her hand out to help Jessica up. "Come on, let's go find my dad and get this party going!"

Jessica couldn't believe the expression on her twin's face when she and Annie Sue strolled out from behind the stable, arm in arm. It was almost worth everything they had been through, she thought happily, to see Elizabeth's look of astonishment.

She could hardly wait to tell her sister everything that had happened since she had sneaked away from Five Elms earlier that evening!

Fifteen

By ten-thirty the spontaneous party at the Sawyers' house had gotten under way. The Sawyers had a wonderful old-fashioned jukebox in the basement of the farmhouse they owned just outside of town, and the refinished basement was a perfect place for dancing. At first Annie Sue's mother was so upset to learn about the girl's close call that she didn't seem to understand what had happened, but once they had explained it all carefully, she couldn't stop hugging Jessica and Alex. She insisted on bringing out platefuls of brownies, cookies, and cold soft drinks for the whole gang. Annie Sue and Dennis had rounded up most of the young people in town in less than an hour, and the Sawyers' basement was crowded with three generations of Walkersville people, all dancing, eating, and having a wonderful time. It was a new experience for the twins to be at a party with people of all ages present, and they both liked it. It was fun to see people their parents' age—and older—dancing and having a good time!

"Hey, everyone!" Annie Sue exclaimed, standing up on a chair and hitting a glass with a spoon to get the crowd's attention. "I have a special announcement to make if you'll all bear with me." Everyone clapped, and Annie Sue blushed. "Seriously," she said. "I want to do two things tonight, and I promise I won't be as long-winded as I usually am. The first thing is, I want to thank Jessica Wakefield publicly for saving my neck tonight. If it hadn't been for Jessica's quick thinking, and fantastic horsemanship, I might have been thrown and terribly hurt." A hush fell over the crowd. "I think most of you know all of this by now. What most of you don't know, though I think some of you do"—Annie Sue smiled meaningfully at Dennis, Hank, Mary, and Carol—"is that Jessica had very little reason to want to help me out tonight. I had a number of opportunities to make Jessica and Elizabeth feel welcome this past week, and instead I made them feel un-wanted."

Mr. and Mrs. Walker exchanged glances. Each put an arm around one of the twins.

"Not only was *I* mean to them, but I convinced my friends to snub them, too. I want to take this opportunity to add a gigantic apology to my gigantic thank you to Jessica *and* to her sister Elizabeth. I know it's a case here of too little and too late, but I hope they'll both accept my warmest wishes—and genuine welcome to Walkersville!"

A roar of applause went up through the crowd.

Then Annie Sue tapped once more on the glass. "Listen, I hate to interrupt, and I promise this is the last thing I'll say," she declared. "But I also want to introduce you all to Alex Parker, the guy who helped Jessica rescue me. I think he deserves a big round of applause and a big thank you, too!"

"I think we have some serious talking and reconsidering to do," Mrs. Walker said to Jessica. "Is that the young man you've been speaking of so highly?"

Jessica grinned. "Isn't he *adorable?*"

Mrs. Walker pressed her heart with her hand. "Well—I don't know about that, dear. But he seems like a very nice young fellow. I think your uncle and I may have been a little hasty in our decision to—"

"Hooray!" Jessica shrieked, throwing her arms around her aunt's neck and giving her an enormous hug. "You mean Liz and I can go tomorrow night with Alex and Brad?"

"I think we need to talk about it, dear," her aunt said. "We haven't met Brad yet, have we?"

"But I need to let Alex know *tonight*," Jessica wailed. "Please," she added, turning to her uncle. "I know you'll really like them both once you get a chance to meet them. Let's go talk to Alex right now."

"Oh, dear," Mrs. Walker said, patting her hair nervously. "I had no idea—I just don't know how your mother can stand the strain. You girls—"

"I wonder where Brad is tonight," Jessica said suddenly, staring at Elizabeth. "Did he say anything about baby-sitting for Evie?"

Elizabeth shrugged. "I'm not really sure," she admitted. She had not yet had a chance to explain to Jessica that her feelings for Brad had cooled considerably over the past couple of days. Still, it would be nice to finish off their vacation with the double date they'd planned. But Brad hadn't been at the fair earlier and wasn't present at Annie Sue's, either. Apparently there would be no opportunity to introduce him to their aunt and uncle.

"Well, come meet Alex, anyway," Jessica said, grabbing her aunt's and uncle's hands and tugging at them. "The minute you talk to him you'll realize how wonderful he is, and that you'd absolutely trust us to go out tomorrow night. And you'll realize that his twin brother Brad is the same kind of guy he is—sweet, dependable, kind . . ."

Her uncle laughed. "Jessica, you ought to go into politics!" he exclaimed. "I feel like the next time I have to run for mayor I'd like you to organize my campaign. When you get behind someone, you really get behind him, don't you?"

"I can't help it," Jessica said. "I guess I get a little excited from time to time."

"You know, we still haven't said anything about your slipping off to the fairgrounds tonight without telling us," her aunt reminded her, looking stern.

Jessica paled. "I'm sorry," she whispered. "I guess Elizabeth and I are used to things being run a little bit differently at home. I really didn't mean to break the rules, but—"

Her aunt smiled and patted her on the arm. "I guess your uncle and I have been a little strict," she admitted. "The last time we had a teenager stay with us was when your mother came at your age. That was a whole generation ago! No wonder we're a little bit rusty." She gave Jessica a hug. "I'll tell you what," she said. "We'll forgive you for sneaking out of the house if you'll forgive us for being too strict for the past week."

"That," Jessica declared, her eyes sparkling, "is a deal!"

Suddenly it seemed that everything was going to work out perfectly. She could hardly wait to introduce them, and later she would tell Alex the wonderful news about the square dance the next night!

"You were just incredible on Midnight tonight," Alex said admiringly to Jessica later. "When I heard Annie Sue start yelling, my stomach hit the ground. I don't think I've ever been so frightened. If he had thrown her . . ." He shuddered. "Jess, you were very brave."

"I guess it was just adrenaline or something," Jessica said. "To tell you the truth, if I'd stopped to think, I don't think I could have even gotten within a foot of Midnight. It all seems kind of amazing now, looking back on it." She wound a silky blond lock around one finger and looked up at Alex from lowered lashes. "Anyway, there's one really lucky consequence to this whole thing—I mean, apart from Annie Sue being OK and making up with us and everything," she added hastily. She didn't want Alex to think she sounded callous after she'd impressed him as being so good-hearted and selfless.

"What's that?" Alex asked curiously.

"My aunt and uncle have decided you're OK now," Jessica informed him. "In fact, they think you're more than OK. They've been running around telling everyone how brave you are, and what a fine upstanding young man you are, and how you're studying agriculture at college and will probably revolutionize farming in Kansas and all that sort of thing."

"Wow," Alex said, grinning.

"But don't you see," Jessica said, "that means that we can start *really* seeing each other now. We don't have to sneak around anymore. And at least tomorrow we can spend the whole day together and then double date with Liz and Brad at the square dance."

Alex looked slightly uncomfortable. "That sounds great," he said weakly.

"And," Jessica added, delighted, "you've sold Midnight now, so you'll have all day tomorrow, won't you?"

Alex thought for a minute. "Yeah, I guess so," he said. "I guess I will."

"But the very best thing is that our double date can still take place," Jessica concluded happily. "Liz and I were feeling so bad tonight, because when we told them about our plans, our aunt and uncle said we absolutely could *not* go. It seemed so unfair when we'd all been counting on it for so long." She clasped Alex's hand in hers. "Won't it be fun? You and Brad and Liz and I going out together at last?"

Alex coughed and looked uncomfortable. "Uh, Jess—" he began.

"Look, there's Liz, talking to Annie Sue over in the corner." Jessica tugged on Alex's hand. "Let's go talk to her about what time we're going to meet and everything. I think we should go out first to the most typically Kansas place you can think of for a big dinner. And then—" She broke off, staring down at his hand. "Hey, what happened to you? Did you cut yourself tonight?" she asked, opening his palm and examining the bandage on his hand.

"Nah. It's nothing," Alex said, jerking his hand away.

Jessica stared at him. He had a strange expression on his face, and for the first time she had a sense that there were things about Alex Parker that she didn't know. The look in his eyes made her decide to drop her questions about his hand. Maybe it was just that he didn't like admitting he'd hurt himself, she thought, shrugging it off.

"Come on. Let's go find Liz," she said. She turned away and moved expertly through the crowd.

Alex paused for a second before following her. Then, taking a deep breath and putting his hand in the pocket of his jeans, he crossed the room to the spot where Jessica was joining Elizabeth and Annie Sue.

Elizabeth was having a wonderful time. It was the first evening since they'd arrived in Kansas that she had felt totally relaxed. Her concern about Jessica had subsided now that their aunt and uncle had relented about Alex.

Her anxiety about Brad was gone now that she realized her brief attraction to him hadn't been of any consequence. More than anything else, she was relieved that the tension they had perceived over and over again between the Walkersville girls and themselves seemed to have vanished. Elizabeth had felt terrible about the treatment they'd received from Annie Sue and her friends. It was a new experience for her to be excluded and to find every friendly overture on her part rebuffed. That night made all the difference in the world. Getting a chance to get to know Annie Sue and her friends made her see everything in a different light. She was enjoying the girl's company. After Annie Sue's public apology and formal welcome to the twins, the brunette had approached Elizabeth privately to explain some of the things she had shared earlier with Jessica.

"Do you forgive me?" she asked Elizabeth earnestly when she had attempted to explain some of the reasons for her behavior.

Elizabeth laughed. "Of course I forgive you!" Her eyes softened. "That speech you made took a lot of guts, Annie Sue. It isn't easy to admit you've behaved badly. Especially in front of a huge crowd!"

"Well, at least we can all relax now and have a wonderful time at the square dance," Annie Sue said. "You two are planning on coming, aren't you?"

"As a matter of fact, we are," Elizabeth said. She was about to explain their plans to double-date when Jessica came up, with Alex following just behind her. "Annie Sue was just asking if we're planning to go to the square dance," she explained to Jessica.

"That's exactly what I wanted to talk to you about!" Jessica exclaimed. "What kind of stuff do people wear to it?" she asked Annie Sue.

"That depends," Annie Sue said thoughtfully. "Some people wear kind of traditional outfits, big full skirts and petticoats, really bright colors, bandannas, and stuff. Other people just come in regular clothes. You can really wear whatever you like."

"Wow," Jessica said, her eyes lighting up. "I'd sure love to find a gingham dress like you always see girls wearing in Westerns."

Annie Sue laughed. "I've got about three dresses like that. Do you want to borrow one?"

Jessica looked ecstatic. "That would be great!" she squealed.

"Yeah," Annie Sue said with a giggle. "A real turnabout, right?"

Soon both girls were convulsed with laughter as they planned which articles of clothing and jewelry they would exchange. Elizabeth stood by, smiling uncertainly at them. Alex looked lost.

"I think I'm missing something here," he said finally.

Jessica looked as though she was thinking about trying to explain, but gave up. "Never mind," she said to him. "It's just kind of a private joke between Annie Sue and me." She looked thoughtfully at Alex. "We still have to figure everything out, like where we're going to meet, what we're going to do about dinner—all that stuff."

Alex shrugged. He still had his hand in his pocket, and he looked slightly uncomfortable.

"Is your hand bothering you?" Jessica asked, leaning forward and touching his wrist as if she were trying to pull his hand out of his pocket. Alex flinched, pulled back, and didn't answer at first.

"No. It's fine," he said shortly.

"What happened to your hand?" Annie Sue asked. "Did you hurt yourself tonight? Let me see it, Alex."

A dark red blush began to spread slowly from Alex's neck across his face. "It's nothing," he repeated helplessly, glancing quickly at Elizabeth out of the corner of his eye. Then, when it became apparent that Annie Sue and Jessica weren't going to let him off the hook, he slowly withdrew his hand from his pocket, quickly showed them his bandaged palm, and tucked the hand under his other arm, avoiding Elizabeth's gaze.

Elizabeth started. Her stomach felt as if she were in an elevator that was dropping too quickly. She stared hard at Alex, scrutinizing the side of his face, the set of his jaw, the outline of his brow. It wasn't possible. Or was it?

The events of the previous week came flooding back to her in a new light. The uncanny resemblance between the two brothers—who were literally *identical* in appearance. The peculiar conflicts in schedules that prohibited either from appearing with the other. It struck Elizabeth then that she'd been feeling as if something were wrong each time she saw Brad. But she couldn't put her finger on it.

Now, seeing the cut on Alex's hand, she knew what it was. The cut was just where Brad had cut himself on the corral gate. Elizabeth realized now that it hadn't been Brad at all.

Because there was no Brad.

"Listen, we're going to go upstairs and look at some of Annie Sue's dresses," Jessica said to Alex and Elizabeth. "Why don't you two try to figure out the best plan for tomorrow night?" She gave Alex a quick kiss on the cheek before slipping off with Annie Sue, leaving Elizabeth alone with him. Elizabeth's heart hammered as she lifted her gaze to meet his.

"Liz—" Alex began.

"Just tell me one thing," she said, her voice trembling with anger. "What's your real name, Brad or Alex? Or is it some other name altogether?"

"It's Alex," he said miserably, staring at the floor. "Liz, I'm *so* sorry. I feel like the biggest jerk in the entire world. Will you give me a chance to explain?"

"I don't really see what possible explanation you could have for lying to us," Elizabeth said, trying to control herself. "How could you possibly do something like this? It's bad enough leading me on," she added. "But what about Jessica? She's really fallen for you!" She stared at him, shaking her head again. "Or half of you, anyway."

"Liz, *please* let me explain," Alex begged.

"I'm sorry," Elizabeth said coldly. "I really don't feel like talking to you right now. But don't worry, Alex. I'll keep your secret from Jessica. You just figure out some way to explain where Brad is tomorrow night, and I'll go along with whatever you say."

Alex looked gratefully at her and began to speak, but Elizabeth cut him off.

"It isn't for your sake," she said pointedly. "It's because I love my sister. And the sad thing is, I think she's crazy enough to be in love with you!" With that retort she spun on her heel and hurried across the room to join her aunt and uncle, leaving Alex Parker staring after her, his face pale and his blue eyes sad.

Sixteen

"I can't believe we're leaving tomorrow," Jessica said sorrowfully, shaking out the red and white gingham dress she had borrowed from Annie Sue and holding it up to herself in front of the mirror. The twins were in their bedroom at Five Elms, getting ready for the square dance. In the end the party at Annie Sue's had gone until almost midnight, and they had both slept late that morning. Elizabeth had spent the afternoon taking a walk with her aunt and uncle while Jessica met Alex at the carnival.

"Alex and I had the most fantastic afternoon together," she said, slipping on the full petticoat that went underneath the gingham dress. "Liz, I know you're going to think I'm being a dope, because I don't usually get serious about guys. But I honestly think things are different with Alex."

Elizabeth looked at her carefully. "Did you two—uh, did you have any kind of serious talk this afternoon?"

Jessica shook her head. "Not really. I mean, we talked about trying to get together again someday, but I'm not sure how likely that is. Kansas and California are so far apart." She wrinkled her nose. "And you know how I feel about long-distance relationships!"

Elizabeth laughed. Her sister had never made any attempt to hide her skepticism about loving someone who was far away. "Listen, after ten days away from Jeffrey I almost agree with you," Elizabeth said. "I can't wait to see him again, though I'll be sad to leave Walkersville," she added hastily, seeing Jessica's face fall.

Elizabeth couldn't help feeling disturbed that Alex hadn't confessed to Jessica that afternoon. It seemed to her to be a bad sign, and she didn't want to encourage Jessica's professions of love for him. The whole thing puzzled Elizabeth. She couldn't figure out why he would play that kind of trick on them.

But Elizabeth had promised Alex she'd keep quiet about it, and she did not intend to break her word. Jessica would never forgive her if she shattered her illusions about Alex.

"You know, you and Brad don't really seem as close now as you did earlier this week," Jessica mused. "Aren't you the teensiest bit excited about our date tonight?"

Elizabeth blinked. So Alex hadn't come up with an alibi yet for "Brad"! "I'm looking forward to it," she said matter-of-factly. "But the truth is, I just like Brad as a friend. It's not like you and Alex at all."

"Will you zip me up, Liz?" Jessica asked, spinning around and lifting up her hair to expose the long zipper on the back of her dress.

"At least everything's OK between Annie Sue and us," Elizabeth said thoughtfully. "That party last night was fun, don't you think?"

"Mmmm," Jessica murmured. "Thanks," she added, pulling away when Elizabeth had zipped her. She hurried over to the mirror to inspect herself. "I look exactly like those girls always do in the movies!" she exclaimed, delighted. The skirt of the gingham dress stood away from her body, held out by the crinoline petticoat. The bodice fit very close, accentuating her slim waist and torso and the neckline plunged just low enough to look good—but not so low as to raise an objection from their aunt and uncle.

"You look fantastic!" Elizabeth said. She had decided to wear something simpler that night, a slim-cut denim skirt and a red and white checked cotton blouse. A bright bandanna tied around her neck completed the look.

"Girls!" their aunt called, opening the bedroom door this time without even knocking. "Come on outside. Uncle Herman wants to take pictures of you to send home to your parents!"

Mr. and Mrs. Walker were planning to come to the square dance later in the evening. After a long talk with Elizabeth on their walk, they had agreed that the girls could do as they pleased that evening, as long as they were back before midnight. Now that they had met Alex and seen how nice he was, they didn't object at all, and they were willing to believe Brad was every bit as nice as his brother. "Oh, every bit," Elizabeth had assured them with a wry smile.

"We're going to miss having you girls around," their aunt said sadly as the twins' uncle snapped their pictures on the porch. "Do you have any idea how much fun it's been for us having you here?"

"You mean we haven't been too much trouble?" Jessica asked.

"Well, we *were* a little concerned about your fatigue earlier this week. But you seem much better now," Mrs. Walker remarked. "Maybe it's love, Jessica. Did you ever think of that? I once read in a book somewhere that when you first fall in love you can either start sleeping much more or much less. I can't remember which."

"Maybe," Jessica said, winking at Elizabeth.

Elizabeth sighed heavily. She just wished Alex Parker were more trustworthy. It seemed ironic to her that she and Jessica had fought all week to convince their aunt and uncle to give them more freedom. Now that Jessica had finally wrangled it, she had permission to go out with Alex.

Everyone thought he was wonderful. Everyone but Elizabeth. Elizabeth didn't think he was wonderful at all.

She just hoped he wouldn't hurt Jessica. She was going to do everything in her power to insure he didn't!

"Alex!" Jessica exclaimed, hurrying down the front walk to kiss him on the cheek. Even Elizabeth thought he looked wonderful. He was wearing denim overalls and a wonderful plaid flannel

223

shirt that was mostly bright yellow, with red and royal blue and a tiny bit of hunter green. His hair was slicked back, and a tiny cowlick popped up in back. He looked scrubbed and shiny, and he had a big bouquet of daisies in his arms, which he divided into three parts, giving one bunch to Mrs. Walker and the others to the twins.

"But where's Brad?" Jessica asked, looking confused.

"Oh, he's really sorry, but it looks like he's not going to be able to make it. He got sick," Alex said. "Liz, he told me to tell you he's *really* sorry."

Elizabeth tried to look surprised and disappointed. "That's a shame," she said, hoping no one noticed how flat her voice sounded. "I hope he doesn't have anything serious."

"I can't believe he's *sick*," Jessica said, staring at Alex. "What's wrong with him?"

"Uh—he's got—what's it called—uh, intestinal flu," Alex said.

"Gracious! That doesn't sound very good," Mrs. Walker said, frowning at Alex. "I hope *you* haven't caught it," she added, her eyes beginning to cloud with worry.

"Oh, no, not me. I'm perfectly healthy. It's

such a strange thing, because whenever there's something going around, it always seems like Brad gets it," Alex said, blushing furiously.

"Poor Liz," Jessica said unhappily. "It's not going to be much fun going on a double date when half the date doesn't show."

"That's all right," Elizabeth said. "I'm sure it's better this way anyway."

Everyone stared questioningly at her, and she cleared her throat. "You know," she added quickly. "I mean, if he has intestinal flu."

"Well, maybe we should get going," Jessica said, looking at Alex's car. "But I still think it's awfully unfair to poor Liz. Who's she going to dance with?"

"I'll just be part of the stag line," Elizabeth assured her sister, giving her aunt and uncle a quick kiss goodbye before clambering into the car with Jessica and Alex.

"See you girls later!" Mr. Walker called, waving.

As Elizabeth settled into the backseat, she had a mean little smile on her face. It suddenly occurred to her that she might give Alex a dose of his own medicine without letting Jessica in on his secret. If she understood what had happened at all, Alex had pretended to be twins because he hadn't been able to decide which of them he preferred. By pretending to be two guys, he'd been able to date both of them for a while.

Well, the way Elizabeth saw it, Alex had his dream evening ahead of him now. He had both Wakefield girls as his dates.

Only Elizabeth intended to make Alex see that two Wakefield girls were too much for anyone, even Alex Parker. And the way to do it was to employ her new-found ally, Annie Sue Sawyer.

Town hall looked like something out of a movie when the twins and Alex entered the front door. It had been transformed. The big room upstairs had been piled with hay, and a caller was positioned at one end of the room. The musicians sounded lively as they tuned up, and the place was filled with Walkersville residents, everyone from senior citizens to small children, all gathered for an evening of music and entertainment. The food, heaped on tables, was country food at its best, luscious cakes of every description, jugs of apple cider and ginger beer, delicious homemade bread, and cheese and sausages—all to keep energy levels up once the dancing got under way.

Elizabeth was in the corner of the room, talking earnestly to Annie Sue. Within minutes she had explained the situation with Alex, making Annie Sue promise she would never breathe a word of it to anyone. "So here's the plan," she said, giggling. "We want Alex to see how awful it can be to have two dates at the same time. Every time you see him dancing with Jessica, go and whisper to him that I'm dying to dance with him. And as soon as he's dancing with me, tell him the same about Jessica. I'll play along and act like I'm really interested in him, as long as Jessica doesn't see what's going on. Between the two of us, Annie Sue, we should be able to drive him crazy!"

Annie Sue grinned. "Sounds like it," she admitted. "I think he's a skunk for pulling this on you two," she added. "I hope you teach him a lesson, Liz."

"Well, we'll see," Elizabeth said quietly. "As long as we don't hurt Jessica, we ought to be able to give Alex back a dose of his own medicine and make him realize he can't mess with people the way he did this past week!"

"OK," Annie Sue said, giving Elizabeth a

thumbs-up sign, "let's get the show on the road. I don't know about you, but I'm ready to make Alex Parker sorry he ever saw double!"

Elizabeth giggled. The music was just beginning, and it was as good a time as any to get started.

Elizabeth was having a wonderful time! First and foremost, the square dancing itself was fun. The townspeople seemed to get a kick out of the fact that the twins were novices, and they made the caller bark out special instructions, such as "Jessica, *swing* your partner, don't just hug him!" Within minutes the twins were able to swing, promenade, and exchange partners with the rest of the Walkersville experts. But that wasn't the only aspect of the square dance that was giving Elizabeth delight. Her plan to embarrass Alex was working perfectly. No sooner did Alex put his arms around Jessica than Annie Sue would go up to the couple, tap Alex on the arm, and whisper that Elizabeth was partnerless. Could he just dance one tiny little dance with her? Under the circumstances Alex wouldn't have dreamed of refusing. As soon as he took Elizabeth up on her request, Annie Sue would be back, this time with a request from Jessica. This constant alternation was made even more difficult by the square-dance configurations, which demanded staying with one partner for at least ten minutes at a stretch. More than once Alex had embarrassed himself by breaking up a dance to rescue one twin or the other. Finally it looked as if he couldn't take any more.

"OK, Liz," Alex said. It was almost ten-thirty, and he looked exhausted. Annie Sue was clearly making him so nervous he couldn't relax and enjoy himself. Fortunately, Jessica seemed to have no idea what was happening. She seemed to assume that Elizabeth wanted a lot of attention because Brad hadn't shown up.

But by that point of the evening Alex had had it. Grabbing Elizabeth by the arm, he pulled her out onto a small balcony overlooking the square below. "Liz, are you trying to drive me crazy?" he gasped.

Elizabeth smiled. "Yep," she said, crossing her arms and studying him thoughtfully.

"Why? Because I made such an idiotic mistake?"

Elizabeth thought for a minute. "I guess because you never apologized for your 'mistake,' " she said. "The way I see it, you lied to us because you couldn't decide which of us you wanted to go out with, so you thought you'd spend some time with both of us. I thought I'd try making your dream come true."

Alex looked pained. "I don't suppose you'll give me a chance just to try to explain," he pleaded.

"Go on," Elizabeth said, relenting. She was getting tired of trying to provoke him, and her natural tendency was to forgive whenever possible. She *wanted* to forgive Alex, but she couldn't imagine thinking highly of him again.

"Well, here goes nothing," he said, looking miserable. "Liz, I did a crummy thing when I met you girls. And pretty much for the reason you suspected. I thought you were both incredibly cute, and I could instantly tell how different you were. I liked you both. And the truth is, I sort of *am* two different people. None of the stuff I told you when I was pretending to be Brad was a lie. I *do* write poetry. And I *do* love to hike. I just also love riding and horses, too. Most of the time I'm outgoing, kind of brash, the way Jessica thinks I am. But I have another side. I guess I was just acting out a fantasy, being one side of myself or another." He sighed deeply. "But I didn't count on one thing."

"What was that? Cutting your hand?" Elizabeth asked.

Alex shook his head. "Sooner or later I knew one or both of you would find out. That wasn't what it was at all. What I didn't count on was falling for Jessica the way I did. With you, well, I like you a lot, Liz. I think you liked me, too, before you started to think of me as a creep. But the chemistry just wasn't right between us. With Jessica it is. Then I was in a bind. As soon as I realized what I was starting to feel for her, I wanted to confess everything. But I thought you'd both end up hating me."

"Alex, listen. I think you've learned your lesson," Elizabeth said gently. "Jessica cares for you a great deal, and I can see you feel the same. I'm not going to torture you any more for a silly mistake." She leaned over and kissed him gently on the cheek. "And I *did* have fun with you this past week—Brad, Alex, or whoever you were." She smiled. "We all have many sides to us. Not even identical twins are immune, I'm afraid."

"You're a good kid, you know that?" Alex said huskily.

"Now go back in and show my sister the time of her life!" Elizabeth ordered. She smiled as she watched Alex turn and walk back inside. She wasn't sure she really understood exactly why he'd done what he had done, but it didn't matter that much anymore. He was obviously sorry, and he obviously cared for Jessica a great deal.

What seemed to matter then was that Jessica and Alex would have a wonderful last evening together. And Elizabeth intended to have a wonderful time, too. It was their last night in Walkersville, and she wanted to make sure she'd remember it forever!

The twins were roaring with laughter as the last dance of the evening drew to a close. "Square dancing is really hard work!" Elizabeth gasped as she and Dennis skipped arm in arm down the corridor formed by dancers on either side of them.

"Swing your partners, do-si-do!" the caller shouted, and mayhem broke out while the townspeople swung each other around and around, breaking into applause when the music ended. Alex gave Jessica a big hug. The applause swelled as Mr. Walker went up to the dais and picked up the microphone.

"I guess you all know this is a bittersweet evening for my wife and me," he said, clearing his throat. "It's sweet because we're with our closest friends, celebrating a wonderful week-and-a-half with our two beautiful nieces. And it's bitter because their visit is drawing to a close. I just want to take this moment to tell them how much we love them and how special their visit has been to us."

This speech met with such tremendous applause that the twins almost had to put their hands over their ears. "Speech! Speech!" Everyone started yelling, stamping his feet, and clapping.

But neither Elizabeth nor Jessica could have expressed what was in her heart just then. They could only hug their aunt and uncle, their eyes shining with tears.

It had been the most wonderful visit, and they knew that for the rest of their lives they would cherish the memories of their precious time in Walkersville.